"*Colorado Mandala* comes from poet Brian Heffron, who departs from his established genre with a novel of the seventies recommended for fans of literary fiction. The novel opens with an eloquent preface explaining the author's early attraction (at age twelve) to hitchhiking, an occupation that leads to journeys throughout America...Its dialogue and descriptions are exquisite, pairing a sense of place with a sense of character and linking the two with a fine mesh of intricate, accurate and sensual description....Heffron's use of the first person is an added bonus, taking full advantage of the protagonist's observations of and experiences with his world and its various interactions, and will delight readers looking for a 'you are there' feel in their reading....There are cave explorations and cockfighting, there's debt and repayment, wilderness encounters, and the coming together of different peoples and personalities - all set against the backdrop of Colorado's natural wonders.

As the story evolves, readers become immersed in the journey, changing relationships between very different protagonists, and an evolving pressure of past upon present which eventually transforms lives and personalities alike...Gripping writing, solid descriptions of friendships, relationships and changes, and the vivid setting of Colorado's wilderness byways: these facets make **Colorado Mandala** a tapestry of light, sound and color perfect for readers seeking evocative, compelling stories of journey and inspiration."

--- Diane Donovan, Senior Reviewer, Midwest Book Review ©

"**Colorado Mandala** is an intricate chain of literary fiction linking...poetic verse with gritty contemporary dialogue and solves conflict with love...The plot is eclectic. Conflicts are resolved in a true to life way... this work may quite likely be genius..."

--- Natasza Waters
--- In D'Tale Magazine ©

"Brain Francis Heffron's novel, Colorado Mandala is a classy looking book with a cover...painting by William Keith of a wild mountain canyon with a distant river. It sets the tone for the book...There's lots of plot...I recommend this book to all who wish to revisit the 1970's..."

--- David Willson, Vietnam Veterans of America, Books in Review II ©

"In cosmic terms, I came of age just 'up the street' from where this book takes place. Several hundred miles north, a few dozen east, and about the time that the war in Vietnam officially ended. It was a time of peace, love, and long hair—lots of long hair. A time that I still miss, after 40 years. So, I may be a bit biased, when it comes to the subject matter of this novel. *Colorado Mandala* tells the story of three very typical people of that time and place. If you lived in Colorado in the 70s, you knew someone just like them: the 'Nam vet, the long-haired rock climber, and the hippie chick. Money was handy, but few of us managed to hold on to any for very long. We shared what we had and looked after each other.

Heffron speaks with the voice of my memories. One can see, hear, taste what it was like to simply be, on the edge of the mountains when love was free, most of us ... indulged ourselves, and we celebrated the gifts of nature. But life wasn't as simple as we try to remember.

Like the characters, I knew men who served. And who came back ... changed. They were difficult to know, hard to love, and haunted in ways that I'll never understand. *Colorado Mandala* is the only book I've read that feels as though it 'gets' it. If you were there, this story is like traveling back to your youth. For everyone else, Heffron's words will take you where we few, we privileged, came of age."

---Julie G Hughes©,
blog.jmarkafghans.com/

"In the preface of this book, author Brian Francis Heffron begins with a tale of how as a young man, he hitchhiked across North America to see its many sights. Traveling free across the country and telling drivers anything that made the ride more exciting.

"Each new ride and new car was a new audience and got a new fable about who I was and where I was going," he writes.

The story he relates from there, however, focuses more on love—something that is also free and needs to be shared with everyone…And it certainly is a tender story that involves both brotherly love and true devotion from an exceptional woman—a woman he affectionately refers to as the girl with the **Colorado Mandala**….But with love comes other human emotions including jealousy, anger, mistrust and even revenge. The author weaves these human frailties into an interesting story that also offers adventure, lust, danger and ultimately true joy.

The story takes place in a rugged but beautiful small town in Colorado and the author's descriptions are spellbinding. Through the voice of character, Paul, one learns of the longstanding friendship between him and a Vietnam War vet named Michael, who has his own demons with which he deals. Paul, on the other hand, is a laid back sort of guy but when he sees Michael's relationship with Sarah unraveling, he is caught between his dedication to his friend and the love that grows for Sarah. The author presents colorful descriptions of these characters as well and it's difficult not to feel for each of them. If you enjoy a good brawl, a frightening adventure or a passionate love scene, you will get all of these and more in this book. It is surely one you won't want to put down until you reach the final page."

--- **Martha Jette©,**
http://mjbookreviews.blogspot.ca/

"A story of love, friendship, and loyalty set in 1970's Colorado. Paul is our narrator as we find ourselves stepping into the lives of two very different men, who are best of friends, our narrator, and Michael, an ex-Vietnam veteran...The writer sets the scenes wonderfully at the beginning of each chapter and the reader is drawn into Colorado life at this time, the characters are so real and descriptions of events and places so vivid, if you close your eyes you could almost *be there!*

But even in the freedom-loving 70s some things cannot ultimately be shared, and feelings cannot always be controlled. Their lives unfold before us, emotions laid bare. Then Paul discovers Michael is keeping a deep secret, kept since his time in Nam, which if told, would change everything. I thoroughly enjoyed reading this book, it has a brilliant story line, which could easily be continued, and as a woman, I especially liked the way it has been told from a man's perspective."

---Susan Keefe©, http://www.susan-keefe.com/

COLORADO MANDALA

MANDALA

A NOVEL

Brian Francis Heffron

LITTLE
HOUSE
BOOKS

Los Angeles, CA

ISBN: 0615760406
ISBN 13: 9780615760407

Library of Congress Control Number: 2013931576
Little House Books, Los Angeles, CA

Copy Editor & Proofreader: Wrexie Bardaglio

Dedicated to John Maguire,
my blood brother,
who has always had my back.

finding in motion what was once in place

PREFACE

W hen I was twelve, I first stuck my thumb out to hitchhike long distance. A yellow Pontiac Bonneville driven by a young Italian girl pulled over onto the dusty shoulder of the Garden State Parkway entrance ramp and I got in. I mention her ethnicity because at that time the Irish and the Italians were like two sides in an ongoing hockey game with lots of checking. I did not really understand this feud other than that as two tribes not yet merged in the American melting pot, they were engaged in a struggle for resources, jobs, opportunities, and that golden fleece: a solid economic future. Then we hippies came along and rejected all that. Things have never been the same since.

Forever after that first free ride, I could almost never be dissuaded from hitchhiking to any destination that had a highway, or any paved road, leading to it. Seventy dollars was my cash threshold to have on hand to set off on a long hitchhiking journey. With seventy dollars in my pocket in Boston, I could be in the Florida Keys for every spring break, or the Colorado Rockies as spring turned to summer, both within a few days to a week of hitching. A week living outdoors in an exterior America, where a pickup truck bed is a double bed, where your last ride often offers you a meal and a real bed for the night. A life lived out of doors was once commonplace in America, but now our developed country seems occupied mostly by raccoons, possums and squirrels. Twenty to forty rides later I would arrive at my destination not having spent a cent.

So America's highways held no mystery for me. Their easily understood systems of routes, urban loops, city bypasses and best of all, major cloverleafs, were my friends, even more than they were for the mere drivers who also used them. No driver was ever forced to stop periodically, when a ride ended, to examine the land through which they were passing. Hitchhiking is moving in unplanned and unknown duration hiccups, hopping like a pogo stick in one general direction until you narrow it down to where you actually want to land. The citizens in the cars that picked me up were very nice to me all over our country, so I went wherever I wanted.

The truth is, I love the hulking cement "Jersey barriers" streaming alongside the fast lane, just inches from the rear view mirror, and separating all of us from the on-coming traffic. They are not eyesores to me. They are part of my human infrastructure, my transportation psyche.

At night, along the highway, I love the dirty-brown light from the cheap sodium vapor lamps cantilevered out over the roadway from giant spindle-like aluminum poles.

I love to examine the pointed advice of previous hitchhikers who have carved their thoughts into the gray metal bases of these lights: "This place sucks for hitchin'!", "No rides for four hours! The Rambler USA72!", "Good luck getting out of here, Oct 1976 Bicentennial!" I love the generic green destination signs that hang out over the highway every few miles. A new universal visual language: "Grand Ave One Mile." I adore the cold empty concrete, the cowboy boots and engine-running gas fumes at any decent truck stop in the absolutely dead black middle of the night.

This connection to highways, and journeys on them, may be because I was born the summer Congress passed the Federal Highway Act. I came in with the highways and have actually grown up on them; my New Jersey suburb had a major national highway route running right alongside its border. This meant that total geographic, continental freedom was only one bold, usually cold, thumb ride away.

And so, I'd bundle up, stuff a small pack with an extra T-shirt and jeans and go off into the darkness, hitchhiking out into the enormous bloodstream of 41,000 mapped miles that run all over America. Except for the annual Route 95 south hitch to Florida, for the sun, I focused mostly on the coast- to-coast, east/west highways draped across America's chest like a diverse array of chains and necklaces. The dark slushy snow of industrial Route 80 at the top, the rustic Route 40 bisecting the country along the old Mason-Dixon line, and the sweaty Route 10 loping through the American tropics of the deep south.

America's highways granted me access to our entire country via a long entrance ramp that started right at the edge of my own hometown. Aladdin's carpet was waiting at the end of that black macadam ramp. All I had to do was stick out my thumb and I was off.

I admitted to the world that I needed a ride. I admitted I wanted to travel for free. I admitted I was going on an adventure. And I'll tell you, the world responded. Everyone likes to see another person on an adventure. They wish they were so bold so they admire you. Many people stopped to pick me up. I never waited anywhere for very long.

Exit 172 on the New Jersey Garden State Parkway was my portal to the innards of America. Within a few years, via hitchhiking, almost every remote mountain range, coastal peninsula or midwestern flatland became a destination for me.

I took moonshine with a grizzled hillbilly farmer in Georgia who teased me about my hair, but then drove me twenty miles out of his way to get me back on track. I met breathtakingly beautiful girls camping wild in the Florida Keys with their kitchen utensils delicately suspended in the crooks and branches of a flamboyantly red Royal Poinciana. I met single moms fleeing unhappy homes: Alice had started to not want to stay home anymore.

Hitchhiking was probably scarier for the drivers giving me rides than it ever was for me. In all the thousands of rides I got I never once felt any true sense of threat, fear or danger. A few times, in my naiveté, I got into cars that I later realized I was lucky to get back out of. But mostly it was safe, cheap and fun.

If the driver sounded crazy, then the crazier I pitched my act. No matter how bizarre they became, I always went a bit further: Met nonsense with gibberish. Met psychosis with agitation. Treat crazy people with true respect on their own level and you'll soon make a friend. (But I would stay away from taking a ride in any vehicle once, or presently owned, by a funeral parlor—just a rule of thumb based on one late night ride through a nor'easter in Maine.)

I should say that, right from the start, I never felt any obligation to tell the truth to anyone who picked me up hitchhiking. Each new ride and new car was a new audience and got a new fable about who I was and where I was going. I simply thought that telling the truth to someone who had gone to the trouble of pulling off the highway to pick me up would be a great disservice to that person and would really let them down. These tired and weary drivers wanted and deserved a lively story from me. They were not on an adventure and I was, and it was time to pay for my ticket.

So, for each new ride, I invented a fresh, Paul Bunyan-sized fable about myself and my dire circumstances, troubled past, urgent mission, pursuit by parents (or worse), and so forth. I told them stories that popped their eyes right out of their bourgeoisie heads. I happened to be a very well-trained fibber at the time, and they needed a good story while they drove, so I was really only holding up my end of the bargain.

Out there in the middle of this enormous country of ours soldiers almost always picked you up. When you were stuck in Nowhereville, Indiana on Route 70 it was a lock that if some young man or woman serving our country passed they would pull over their (invariably) American muscle car to give me a ride—or a drive, really, because they always immediately moved over into the passenger seat, and, having judged me capable of handling their huge, overblown, over-horse-powered product of Detroit, they asked me to drive. This was true when I roved America's national boulevards, and I believe it's still true today. American military personnel simply always pick up hitchhikers. Why? Because they have only a few days' leave and it is a long way between their base and their hometown. And so they always want to cover that distance as quickly as is combustion-enginely-possible and hitchhikers who can drive facilitate this speedy process. After they pick you up, these soldiers almost immediately fall deeply asleep, so it is important to identify their ultimate destination before they are overcome with an unwakeable slumber.

I once met a soldier very much like the character Michael Boyd Atman, whom you are about to meet within the pages of this book, when he picked me up hitchhiking on Route 70 in Kansas in the seventies. If this is of any use to you, imagine that Paul, the narrator of this story, actually hitchhiked into our tale by meeting Michael in just this manner, as a hitchhiker thumbing a ride somewhere in the high desert of Route 70 in Kansas or eastern Colorado, heading straight for that bright line of snow-dusted mountains that splits our country from top to bottom like a spine: the Rockies. That mystical meeting between our characters would have had to occur long before our tale begins, when they have already become blood brothers.

This book is about the crazy, glorious and romantic notion that every generation conceives anew: that love can be a spiritual gift shared openly among all who feel it, not coveted, or hidden, or hoarded. Each new generation gradually learns how real life involves loyalty and jealousy, sexual fidelity, and the intimacy that can only grow up between two people.

Each new generation learns that love, in its purest and most universal form, can be shared among more than just two people and that therefore we can, and should, all simply love each other unhindered in the here and now.

The story is my own. The characters are my own as well. Both the plot and the people lived once in a time of tenderness, rebellious music, and long hair that was quite different from our times now.

But do not worry, I will not go on and on about how great it was back then. I will simply say, knowing you as I do, dear reader, that you might very well have enjoyed living back then. Yes. I feel certain that you would have liked it very much.

Brian Francis Heffron
March 1, 2013

Chapter I

A narrowing canyon: deep, long and slim, with fluted columns of red sandstone and brickish dented walls. Yellow cinquefoils blooming from niches bob in the noonday breeze. Within the canyon is a fast stream so filled with rocks and boulders that the water can hardly find a course. The bank is clay and has retreated with the burden of the spring run-off. Along the southern shore is a roadbed; beside it a flock of brewer's blackbirds feed on ticks and water spiders. Their hollow white eyes snap-to at the first rumble of an approaching vehicle.

Red dust, clouds of it, rose like a plume from the back of the jeep. Michael Boyd Atman was sitting on one side of the open tailgate with Stuart Jr., the kid on the other. Between them lay the pup, Strider, on his side panting. They had to keep their eyes closed tight against the clouds of red dust, but occasionally Michael would open his for a quick glance across the stream, his eyes always alert and on the swivel, observing and absorbing everything with a military precision. We were just entering the canyon and here the far bank sloped up steeply, completely covered with thin bristlecone pines.

I didn't know where I was going, but that really didn't matter. The rutted roadbed was unyielding to my steering, and the dried mud creases held the wheels like a slot car. Driving was more like being a switchman, choosing the route by the ruts at all points of decision. Beside me sat Michael's girlfriend and the kid's mother, Sarah, smoking a long thin cigarette. The shapely supple muscles of her slim arms tensioned and loosened, holding on tight to the jeep as we veered back and forth in concert with the canyon.

We came around a bend and the canyon was suddenly filled with Cub Scouts—dozens of them on both sides of the road, carrying plastic garbage bags and running around cleaning the place up. On the bank near the water was a mountain of filled sacks. The scouts were all grinning at us and giving us the peace sign.

"They look like little beavers building a dam," said Sarah.

The pines began to yield to rock, tall and speck-led cliffs, seventy feet up and overhanging. We were now in the South Platte River canyon. Ahead, three fishermen, all in tall olive waders, splashed around in the stream like bird dogs. They looked up as we passed, frowning at the noise of our jeep, as if their own commotion hadn't already scared every trout for five miles. One of them, the smallest, gave us the fin-ger; the kid thought it was a new kind of peace sign so he flashed it right back. The guy must have felt great getting the finger from a little kid. Michael sat up be-tween the front seats and looked out. Except for his long twirling hair, you might think Michael was still in the Army. Even now, years after leaving Viet Nam, his jaw still retained the clean-shaven, sharply defined line of a Special Forces military man. Beads of sweat dripped from his strongly aquiline face.

"The river is a lot lower this year than when I was here last. It was right up to the roadbed then. You can see where it carried off that shack and left it in the sand."

In the middle of the stream on a high sandbar was a graying wood shack on its side, roofless. The paral-lel walls leaned far to one side.

I had never been here before. It was a thinning, dusty canyon. Michael had told me about it the night before at the Loop Lounge.

"How did you hear about this place?" asked Sarah. Glancing over at her, I could see that the apex-noon sun was casting shimmering yellow flecks into her clear green eyes. She was still holding on tight to the jeep with both hands.

"Alan and I came up here last spring and jumped off the cliffs for accuracy. It was great trying to go straight through an inner tube jumping all the way from the top," Michael said. "Too low for that this year, though. Bad luck!"

"Yeah, bad luck," I said with sarcasm. Alan was probably Michael's craziest old Colorado friend. I had been driving up here to this canyon all morning from Manitou Springs so I was looking forward to stretching my legs and uncramping my stiff muscles. Today's boisterous outdoor activities were planned late, late last night at a bar table, which should explain a lot, including my cramped, water-starved muscles.

"This is it," Said Michael. "We're almost there."

The cliffs rose on both sides. On our left, the steep red rocks plunged straight to the road's edge. On the far shore, the cliff face rose sheer from the foaming rapids. The stream thinned and accelerated through this new alley-like narrows. I tried to estimate the depth of the water, to see if it could ever be safe to jump from the top. No, it seemed much too shallow, perhaps from halfway up.

"This is it," said Michael. "Right there, see the white water? Well, it spills out into a slow pool and then you can ride it all the way down."

I slowed down and pulled off the road onto a narrow shoulder where I parked in the shade of an overhanging ledge. The kid, whom I had only met today, took off as soon as I stopped. He hadn't said much during the whole trip up, but just sat smiling. I figured he was shy.

Michael and I were in long pants and had to change. Sarah followed our thirsty dog Strider down to the stream's edge where he drank deeply. I peeled off my jeans and put on my climbing shorts. My legs felt great to be unfettered. After we had both changed we got the truck tire inner tube off the jeep roof and walked upstream high above the water. On a huge boulder along the river we passed about ten Denver teenagers. Almost all of them were wearing sailor's watch caps. They thought that made them look tough; a few were playing guitars, and all were drunk and loud.

We left the road and made our way toward a crack in the cliff. It became a loose shale path leading steeply down to the torrent. Michael hurried down, jumping from rock to smooth rock, all the while rolling the wide inner tube in front of him. He pulled up short of rushing in and slowly dipped his foot into the water.

"Ahhh," he grimaced, "it's freezing!"

Just under six feet tall, Michael was an extremely striking figure. He had a shock of rebellious dirty blonde hair that cascaded to his shoulders. His eyes were an intense shade of flinty gray that shined out from young crows' feet like a lantern light in darkness. His face was like a nervous animal's, moving, twitching, and seemingly always ready for any action. He instantly jumped on the inner tube and paddled out into the fastest part of the current, his back muscles undulating with the effort. He soon left my sight, bouncing down over a roller coaster of white water, yelling.

His husky voice soon faded away in the fleeting foam. The shore's thick dust clung to my feet and itched. I waded in to my knees; the water was chilling cold, a shimmering white reflection of the sky above. The bottom was covered with smooth worry-stone pebbles and sloped away into a sharp V. The stream was about thirty feet across at that point. In the center the current was the slowest, although still fairly fast. The water rushed along both sides of my rapidly numbing and whitening climber's legs. It felt wonderful, and thoroughly purged whatever was left of my hangover. I squatted down and splashed my face in the icy water.

Presently I saw Stuart coming down from the road with the inner tube. He slid like a skier in the loose gravel. His long straight hair was the exact same shade as his mother's. He had a habit of flicking his bangs out of his eyes with a short swift shake of his sandy head.

"Michael said to tell you it's great. He says wait 'til you get past this first narrow part, the next one is even better."

He rolled me the inner tube and I jumped on. I kicked my way out into the current, and it picked me up like a mailbag.

I got comfortable lying on my chest with my arms overhanging. Paddling and kicking, I tried to keep my head facing downstream, but I was soon spinning out of control. Up and down over unseen rocks, my head and shoulders were often buried in the icy water. It was strange not to be able to control the tube with my body, but though sturdy, my climber's muscles were simply no match for this spring stream's swift, solid current. The stream's first pass went up over a rock and then down ten feet over two more. I could see the rich green moss on the faces of the submerged stones. Then the current slowed down, flowing into a small, languid pool. I drifted serenely towards the down-stream exit. Just before I reached the edge, feet first, I heard something that sounded like loud applause. I gradually recognized it was the roar of falling water.

I was powerless. I free-fell for about twenty-five feet, landing partially in the water and partially on a rock. My back stung, tearing as the rock bit in. The inner tube took the worst of the jolt, but I lost my grip and went under.

When I came up, spitting like a whale, the inner tube was only about ten feet away. I swam to it and slowly worked my way on. My legs and arms were bloody, though numb from the cold water. Long abrasions, sprouting droplets of bright red blood, traced torn lines from my shins all the way up to my knees. Once back onto the tube, I floated slowly downstream again towards the red bank nearby. I gradually perceived the sound of a voice yelling over the continuous roar of the water. I looked up and could see Michael high above me on the cliff, laughing and dancing around, and pointing at me, and laughing.

Sarah stood very still with a pool cue in her hands. She had her back to me and a burning cigarette was perched carefully on the edge of the pool table beside her. She was facing the table and it was darker behind her. A silver triangle leapt from her insoles to the division of her legs. Her back was bare, save for the loose knot holding her knitted halter-top, with large macramé stitches revealing glimpses of her gleaming brown skin. She was delicate, yet very strong: the limbs of a dancer. She might be Michael's girlfriend, but she was damn beautiful from the back.

I love delicate, delightful, chick pool players, I thought, drunkenly, they are grace in motion.

Sarah with a long "S."

She was more or less like glass than anything else.

Long legs and short sight.

Her soft sandy hair was now up, coiled carefully into a complex circular bun, spinning slowly back inwards like a mandala. A scent I did not recognize hung in the air around her. Much later I found out it was the alluring fragrance of frankincense. I noticed my breath deepening.

It was about six o'clock, so there were only two tables being used. Everybody else was at the bar. It's funny because all the girls at the tables were fat. What's even funnier is that all the guys at the tables were wearing tennis hats. Two tables of fat girls and white tennis hats bobbing up and down getting drunk. Michael was playing pool with Sarah; he was already drunk on tequila, and she was beating him easily. We'd gotten back into Manitou about four; then after some minor medical work by Sarah, tending to my abrasions and cuts from the river accident, we had come down here to the Loop Lounge and Fireside Room, our dim happy hour home.

The Loop was a cave tavern with a bright door on the dusky avenue. Down the bar, a long-legged cowgirl sipped her Mimosa, wearing a turquoise necklace punctuated with silver. I know because I sold it to her.

In the back, oily smoke twirled above the pool tables. Below, man-boys wearing knives on their belts tilted into billiard shots.

"Hey Paul, what's up?" It was Alan behind me, then sitting down beside me on a barstool. His leg accidentally hit mine beneath the bar and I winced as my fresh scrapes were struck. Alan was another Viet Nam vet and he and Michael had long been friends. Recognizing in each other the face of combat, death, and losses, even here in this mountain utopia, they spoke their own language and no one came between them on anything of importance, including me.

"Nothing, just got back from the canyon."

"Oh, so you did go up there, then! Michael is one hard-case knucklehead. He was so drunk when he promised to go up there that I never thought he'd even remember saying he was going, much less actually driving all the way up there! How was it?"

I was about to point out that Alan was supposed to go with us, but had not answered his door to loud knocking at dawn, and that I had done all the driving, both back and forth, when, without waiting for a reply, he went straight on talking.

"Hey did you hear what happened at the Crystal Palace? Some bikers tore the place up. They threw Windsor through a window cause he tried to stop them. He got stabbed in the face too."

"No kiddin'." I sipped my drink. I knew it was pointless to stand between Alan and a juicy story he had to tell. "How did it start?"

"Well the bikers were getting pretty drunk and very loud, so Windsor simply asked them to quiet down a bit. Soon as he opened his mouth, the whole place went silent. One of the bikers, a really big guy with a teardrop tat beneath his left eye, reached over the bar and grabbed Windsor by the throat. He pulled him completely over the bar and threw him onto a table where some civilians were sitting. Windsor went as red as a fire engine. He lost it and started throwing every glass in sight."

A few people came over to hear Alan's story. I could see Michael standing just outside the pool table light, listening intently, and watching Sarah and me with a drunken grin.

"So this big biker pulls a knife," continued Alan, "and stabs Windsor in the head. As soon as he sees he's bleeding, Windsor goes limp as a prick and they threw him through the front window. Windsor looked terrible lying face down in broken glass on the sidewalk."

There was some laughter and grinning.

"Did the cops bust the bikers?" asked Michael from the shadows. A beer lamp caught and silhouetted the razor-edged profile of his solid jaw-line.

"They got the big guy, but the other two got away. The big one stayed around trying to get Windsor to wake up. I guess he thought he killed him."

His story over, Alan paused, then recognizing Michael as the questioner he called out to him. "Hey Michael, why not give us a poem! You haven't done that in forever."

Michael smiled broadly and without further prodding stepped forward out of the dimness, finding his light in the golden glow of an Olympia Beer lamplight. He looked around at each of the faces of the bar patrons, who were now all turned towards him and paying him rapt attention. He knew them all by name and they all knew him.

"Well, it's been so awful cold at night lately," Michael drawled, "so that brings to mind "The Cremation of Sam McGee" by that dear old friend of mine, Mr. Robert Service."

People got comfortable, cradling their drinks and sinking back in their bar stools. Within seconds they were all under his spell.

"*There are strange things done in the midnight sun,*" Michael began, his whiskey-soaked voice heavy and full.

"*By the men who moil for gold;*
The Arctic trails have their secret tales
That would make your blood run cold;
The Northern Lights have seen queer sights,
But the queerest they ever did see

Was that night on the marge of Lake Lebarge
I cremated Sam McGee."

Michael paused, his flinty eyes darting out at his listeners. Yes, they were ensnared—just the way he liked them. The power of his oratory filled him up. The corners of his mouth curled upwards, and he bared his perfect teeth into a smile he knew his listeners would find intoxicating.

"… He was aaaalways cold," Michael drawled, letting the word lounge in his mouth a bit," but the land of gold seemed to hold him like a spell;

Though he'd often say in his homely way that he'd sooner live in hell.

… And that very night, as we lay packed tight in our robes beneath the snow,

And the dogs were fed, and the stars o'erhead were dancing heel and toe,

He turned to me, and Cap, says he, I'll cash it in this trip, I guess;

And if I do, I'm asking that you won't refuse my last request."

Michael stopped and drained his whiskey glass. Every pair of eyes in that bar bored into him. The women—breathing hard, visibly—and the men, too, were transfixed. Michael took all this in, and then continued.

"Well, he seemed so low that I couldn't say no; then he says with a sort of moan:

It's the cursed cold, and it's got right hold till I'm chilled clean through to the bone.

Yet 'taint being dead—it's my awful dread of the icy grave that pains;

So I want you to swear that, foul or fair, you'll cremate my last remains."

A brief scuffle in the far corner of the bar brought Michael's gaze upward again for a beat. Shadows and light and whiskey tangoed together in his mind for a moment. An old scene seemed to flash there as well. But Michael blinked back the memory, whatever it was; no, not now. He shook it off and continued:

"A pal's last need is a thing to heed, so I swore I would not fail;

And we started on at the streak of dawn; but God! he looked ghastly pale.

He crouched on the sleigh, and he raved all day of his home in Tennessee;

And before nightfall a corpse was all that was left of Sam McGee."

Breathing in the bar had seemingly ceased completely. His audience was all one body, one ear, and one eye. All upon Michael Boyd Atman.

"There wasn't a breath in that land of death, and I hurried, horror-driven,

With a corpse half hid that I couldn't get rid, because of a promise given;

… Now a promise made is a debt unpaid, and the trail has its own stern code.

In the days to come, though my lips were numb, in my heart how I cursed that load.

In the long, long night, by the lone firelight, while the huskies, round in a ring,

Howled out their woes to the homeless snows—O God! how I loathed that thing."

Michael's voice now softened. Something snuck into it that hadn't asked permission, and remained. What was it? His audience saw their performer naked before them and this engaged them even more.

"… Till I came to the marge of Lake Lebarge, and a derelict there lay;

It was jammed in the ice, but I saw in a trice it was called the "Alice May."

And I looked at it, and I thought a bit, and I looked at my frozen chum;

Then "Here," said I, with a sudden cry, "is my cre-ma-tor-eum."

Some planks I tore from the cabin floor, and I lit the boiler fire;

Some coal I found that was lying around, and I heaped the fuel higher;

The flames just soared and the furnace roared— such a blaze you seldom see;

Then I burrowed a hole in the glowing coal, and I stuffed in Sam McGee."

Here Michael stopped again. Had that old memory returned...the one he had tried to push away earlier? Tears welled in his eyes and he felt sheepish, almost frightened, but then—he realized he didn't care. He let it come and the tears fell.

"Then I made a hike, for I didn't like to hear him sizzle so;

And the heavens scowled, and the huskies howled, and the wind began to blow.

... I was sick with dread, but I bravely said: "I'll just take a peep inside.

I guess he's cooked, and it's time I looked";...then the door I opened wide.

And there sat Sam, looking cool and calm, in the heart of the furnace roar;

And he wore a smile you could see for a mile, and he said: 'Please close that door.

It's fine in here, but I greatly fear you'll let in the cold and storm—

Since I left Plumtree, down in Tennessee, it's the first time I've been warm."

Michael's voice softened even further now and his audience bowed their heads unconsciously, leaning in to listen, as if each of his words were now fragile frozen snowflakes that they knew they needed to catch.

"There are strange things done in the midnight sun
By the men who moil for gold;
The Arctic trails have their secret tales

That would make your blood run cold;
The Northern Lights have seen queer sights,
But the queerest they ever did see
Was that night on the marge of Lake Lebarge
I cremated Sam McGee."

Michael stopped, and the shadows that had gathered about his face departed. There was utter silence in the bar and for a moment, Michael thought no one liked it.

But then—pandemonium.

Clapping, cheering, backslapping, drink-buying. Our friends loved the fact that the poem was long and lyrical, but mostly they loved the fact that Michael could recite it completely from memory. It was just beyond anything they could dream of doing and because of that they all loved the guy they called Kentucky Mike, and had since he had first arrived in Manitou—a hard-nosed man from Hazard, Kentucky, who was a hazard himself, a country boy who never failed to surprise with his charm and appealing charisma.

Alan was the first person to reach Michael with a fresh drink. Michael fired down the shot in one motion and then the two vets hugged tightly. It was a private club. By then the bar patron swarm overwhelmed them both and the whiskey and beer chasers flowed.

As I passed I heard Michael tell an interested, flirty young woman, "You may call me a crazy neurotic, baby. But all that means is you can't predict what I am going to do next. I'm just another hippie who can recite a poem but whose tongue gets screwed up in a conflation of weird words if someone that I don't know, like you, approaches. But, among my real friends," and here he began to bob and weave like a boxer, "I'm a bouncing active menace harassing their movements and eventually their thoughts!" Then he chugged the beer the woman had bought him.

I had lost interest. I'd heard all Michael's recitations and post-recitations long before now. I was back watching Sarah and she wasn't listening either. She had already seen that Michael's poetic success was fueling more drunkenness.

I watched as her dancer's form flowed around the pool table taking movie star puffs off her cigarette and making difficult shots, her movements as natural and sensual as a river as it flows around sharp bends in a canyon. She leaned far over the table to make a long double pad shot and I looked up over her back and saw Michael's gleaming eyes looking straight back at me in the darkness. He was staring with a smirk on his red and bruised face.

With one last swift stroke of her pool cue Sarah sank the eight ball. Then straightening up, she smiled to herself. The sweet curve of her breasts and halter rose and fell in satisfied pleasure. She replaced her cue in the rack and came down to join me. Michael went outside.

As if her movements needed any more emphasis, as she walked slowly toward me in the aisle behind the bar stools, she jingled. That is, her bell did. She wore a small round bell hanging out of her jeans' pocket on a leather thong. She made no attempt to silence it as she drifted towards me. In fact, it seemed the slight swing and sway of her hips actually accentuated it. As she approached, the lilting notes of the Doors' song, *Crystal Ship*, sailed out of the jukebox and filled the room with a palpable and soothing sensuality.

"You can play pool pretty well but I doubt you'd beat Michael if he were sober," I said, my breath thick with drink and a taboo desire.

"I'd like to have another kiss," sang Jim Morrison as Sarah sat down and ordered a drink. Then she fixed those huge, tear-shaped green eyes upon mine.

"What's the problem with you and Michael? You're so close, and yet you fight with each other," she asked. "Why fight? It doesn't make any sense."

Listening to her, I was looking through the effects of innumerable beers, ten scotch and waters, and one slightly blackened eye. Then her fragrance wafted over me and calmed my nerves.

"I've never seen him act like such an ass before," she continued. The soothing tones of her sweet voice held me in place like a moonbeam through a skylight.

She lit another cigarette. "He had about a ten ton chip on his shoulder today. He asked for everything he got."

She was missing the point; I liked her and wanted her to get it.

"Sarah, you gotta realize, most of the time he isn't even thinking about what's going on. Sure he's working in it, but he doesn't stop to think about it. He never does, until a long time after. He just gets the spirit and he's off."

I really didn't know how to explain it. Besides, I was feeling too good to care. She looked like a goddess. As natural as the mountains and rivers we lived amidst. I looked at her looking at me and I wanted her. Every climber's muscle in my entire half drunken body tensed as I caught her look and returned it. She flinched quickly under my gaze and looked down into her drink.

"You know what this is?" I held up my money that was lying on the bar. "It looks like money but it isn't, it's rent. It's rent and I'm gonna spend it right now on booze because I don't give a damn. I'll never learn and I'm proud of it."

"You're incorrigible," she said. "And I think you're kidding, too." She smirked and laughed. Then she leaned over the bar to sip from her glass and the half hidden curve of her browned breasts seen through the knitted netting of her halter top teased me until I had to look away.

Not long after that I got to a point where I would have to go home or I was never going to make it. Noticing, Sarah crushed out her butt and spun her stool around to face me.

"Come on, let's go find Michael and head home. We can all stay at my house."

Standing up and helping me to my feet, she wrapped those strong arms around me and we made our way out into the neon-lit street, the last, hard-core patrons calling their good-byes as we passed.

Outside, Michael was sprawled spread-eagled on the hood of the jeep. As we exited, his head rose from the hood and he shook it wildly, his tangled locks spraying out like a twirling mop. Slowly he roused himself. Trying to rise from the jeep hood he fell off into the street.

"You're nothing. You're just my helper," Michael spoke from the gutter. "But stealing my woman? Even a partner can't get away with that. So, it seems I'll have to teach you another lesson."

"Stop it, Michael. Will you grow up?" Sarah pleaded, her voice rising in anger.

Michael pulled himself up by the jeep's bumper. He stumbled over and squared off in front of me. Sarah stepped in between us. I really wanted to hit him.

It happened fast. Michael grabbed Sarah and threw her down. That was it for me. Seeing Sarah crumpled on the pavement was just too much.

But turning back to Michael he hit me hard across the jaw. I took the punch and hit him as hard as I could in the stomach and he screeched and went down instantly, grabbing his gut. He rolled around moaning for a moment, and then he puked.

"Bastard, you bastard!" said Sarah, now sitting on the curb edge of the sidewalk.

You can batter Michael about the skull all night long, but one punch to the gut and he's down, and I knew it. I sat down next to Sarah on the curb and checked for all my teeth with my tongue. My mouth was bleeding, but it didn't seem to hurt too much. I figured it would pretty soon. Sarah put her arm around me and tilted her head over to look me in the face.

"Come with me, we can just go upstairs to my studio. I'll get you cleaned up and you can sleep over. Let's go there now, please."

In the scrap, Sarah's mandala-shaped bun had unraveled so her pale hair now hung down around her face like a halo. It would have taken my breath away, if I weren't already out of breath.

Michael was still rolling around and moaning behind us.

"I can't leave him here. I'll just sit here till I sober up enough to drive, and then I'll take him home. I'm sorry, I'd like to, and God knows he deserves it, but I can't leave him."

She sat there looking at me, needing me to take her away to a safer place, and I suddenly realized a desire for her that I had not felt consciously until that exact moment. I wanted her to wash my face with her gentle, able hands. Wow, is Michael an idiot, I thought.

"Where are the keys?" she asked, and got up to see if Michael had them.

She got them and started the jeep up. I helped her get him into the back, got in front, and we drove away.

During the night a dream: Sarah's head lay on my bare chest, her long hair a blanket. Outside the window, bare branches rocked in the wind. A full moon spotted the night sky like a stage light. The light on Sarah's shoulders was white like the sheen of an apple.

Chapter II

A valley: wide but only a fraction of the window's view, retreating up to the summit. In the first range, the aspen and evergreen are a thick, satiny green. In the second, the hue is grayed by distance. On the last, where rock begins, the trees are sparse and gnarled: one side thick to the sun, the other thin to the wind. In a high glade, a herd of pronghorn sheep feed on stunted vegetation. Their white rumps blend with the snowy rocks as they alternately move and stand still in unison.

As soon as I woke up, I was sorry I did. My jaw ached and one eye was as tender as a burn. I just lay there, aching and trying to focus. Slowly, objects revealed themselves: the bed was high and double-wide, the bedsteads were black ovals. The walls were rough plaster with a rail running all the way around the whole room at eye-level, with pegs in it every so often. Several small, framed paintings hung from it, too. Beside the bed there were only two other pieces of furniture in the room: a Larkin side-by-side, and a frail lady's writing table below the single window.

Outside, I could see the half-moon, pale and fading in the morning sky. The curtains were thin lace, brown with age. They would reach up and into the room with the breeze, and then abruptly suck back to the frame. The mass of the mountains filled the window halfway up.

Restless and shifting, I suddenly became aware of an intimate warmth. Lying fully clothed, except for my mountain boots under a quilt, I rolled over and encountered what I had sensed: a sleeping face, framed by pale, sandy wisps of soft hair and the fine gossamer-silk surface of a nightgown collar.

I came fully awake.

It only took me a few minutes to find the bathroom. I also found Michael downstairs snoring on the couch. What I really wanted though was to shave. I like to shave. Somehow the removal of yesterday's growth also removes a lot of yesterday. Whiskers are fine, I've had one scraggly beard already, but I always wind up waking up some morning wanting to shave it all off.

The atmosphere of the bedroom was narrowed and defined by the bathroom. Whatever this magical ambiance was, it would vanish if Sarah ever departed. She was everywhere. A myriad of miniature bottles lined the shelves. A tiny tube of toothpaste with a brush labeled "Guest" was laid on the edge of the sink. I also found a small vial labeled frankincense and opened it. Here was the delicate and delicious fragrance I had been absorbing all day the day before. Seductive and soothing, it filled my nostrils with pleasure and eased my headache. It was Sarah in a bottle.

There was also a man's razor; I mean a model designed for a man. I soaped up and began to shave. In the mirror, my right eye was cloudy, the white part half-filled with blood. My cheeks were swollen as if puffed out by cotton. Examining my face, I looked up and saw Sarah standing cross-armed in the doorway. The sunlight behind her outlined her lithe body within her silk nightgown in a perfect silhouette.

"You can expect a guest, standing in the doorway like that," I said.

"What do you mean?" she asked, a bit startled.

"Nothing, just a gypsy superstition."

"Oh," she said. "Good morning, Paul. You rose in an awful hurry. I hope there isn't anything wrong."

Sleep was still in the corners of her almond shaped eyes. As she spoke, she balled her fists and rubbed her eyes to clear them.

"Oh no. Just another gypsy superstition. I read that they never greet each other in the morning until they've washed. Even if they literally sleep right next to each other, they ignore each other until they've both washed. I guess because privacy is so minimal, their codes have to be very strict."

I was still shaving.

"Are your codes as strict, Paul?" Her voice carried a huskiness I hadn't heard before. There was a pause.

"Some, I guess," I replied. I couldn't look at her again. I felt way too much yearning within me to touch her, and she was Michael's. I splashed my face with water.

"In that case, I better get washed up too." She turned quickly to go, but trailed one eye to watch my reaction. I smiled into the sink.

"Would you like something to eat? I'd be glad to make you breakfast." The notes of her voice rose at the end, like a climbing piano scale, but also losing volume as she descended the steep cabin stairway. "Pancakes and coffee all right?" echoed up from the first floor.

"Fine," I said, a little anxiously. "Sounds great."

"Michael's asleep down here. We might as well let him sleep in after yesterday."

Yes, I thought, but didn't say anything.

Done shaving, I stood there in Sarah's sweet feminine bathroom, looking at my bruised face in the circle of the un-steamed mirror, thinking suddenly, totally, and completely about yesterday.

CHAPTER III

A house, terraced in among many cabins roosting on the steep hillside. Kitchen windows facing east reflect the sun like yellow eyes. Light filters into this house, through the planters hovering at different levels, in green shafts. Along the windowsill, jelly jars nurture rooting sprouts. A shelf wraps around the other three walls, just above eye-level. It holds food provisions, three deep in each item. In the corner, an unlit wood-burning stove sits on ornate bathtub feet. The walls are knotty pine paneling of irregular widths. Through the top half of the open Dutch door, the sky is the color of a stream frozen in midair, a translucent blue.

Creaky wooden stairs heralded my approach. Like most mountain homes, the passage down was steep and narrow. Sarah was busy at the counter as I entered the kitchen. The first thing I noticed was the smell. It was like an aquarium, only earthier. There were plants everywhere

"There's a good picture," I said, "the pioneer woman at her morning chores."

Sitting down at the table, I saw Stuart outside on his knees with Strider. They were watching two cats fight: a black tom stalking a pure-white female, occasionally catching her. Abruptly, the white took off at high speed, leaving the tom confused and idle.

"Would you build a fire while I get this ready?" Sarah asked. She was making batter and the muscles of her arms stood out prominently in the effort. "I assume you were a Boy Scout when you were young?"

"Hell with that," I said, swinging open the iron door of the stove. "I wasn't a Boy Scout...I was an American Indian."

She smiled and laughed at my weak joke, but again, I couldn't look back. It seemed I just couldn't make myself hold Sarah's gaze this morning. A kind of inner ache accompanied it. The fire flamed quickly, and I sat back down at the table in the chair nearest the window.

Sarah lived high up, close to the top, on Serpentine Drive, a dramatic and beautiful switchback road that scaled the steep series of inclines leading up to Pikes Peak. The road passed behind her cabin, leaving the view clear to see the entire basin with the town of Manitou nestled within it like a toy Christmas village. A fence guarded the back edge of her lot where the land dropped off precipitously to the road far below. Past the highway in the center of the valley, I could see two bright red, building-sized rocks in the Garden of the Gods. Squinting, I could just make out two climbers, strapped with orange belting, scrambling up their virtual vertical faces. I missed climbing and thought I must go again soon.

When Stuart saw me, he came in. He sprung up onto the chair directly across from me and leaned in on his elbows holding his chin in his hands. Michael must have done his clothes shopping, because he looked like his fashion junior; cowboy boots slid out of Stuart's Lee jeans so only the boot toe and heel showed. The rest of the boot was swallowed up within turned up denim cuffs. The sleeves of his black pocket T-shirt made his arms seem like thin pipes.

"Good morning, Mom," he said without looking over at her at the stove.

"Good morning, Stuart," we said, almost together.

"You and Michael must have fought again. You have a new bruise. I wish I'd seen it."

"It was a very short round. Nothing much to see."

"Did anybody win this time?" he asked.

"No, not yet."

"Michael's inside sleeping on the couch," said Sarah.

"I know, Mom. I saw him when I got up. He always sleeps down here when he's too drunk to go up with you."

"Breakfast is served," Sarah interrupted, putting an end to her boy's anxiety.

I looked up at her as she placed a stack of pancakes in front of me on a plate. She gave me a questioning look. Briefly, our eyes held, a tunnel-like concentration, the way you see when you're running very fast. It made up for all the times I couldn't look at her that morning. Sarah returned to her stove to get my coffee.

Suddenly Stuart spoke up in a loud stage-voice. "When is Michael getting up?"

"I don't know, Stuart," Sarah said with her back still turned to both of us.

As I ate, Stuart examined the small areas of my face, noting each new cut or swelling, as if for comparison with Michael, later.

"Stuart, will you let Paul eat his breakfast in peace?"

"All right," he said, climbing quickly down from his chair. "I'll wake up the Big Dog." And with that he stomped out of the kitchen.

"Gee, that's swell!" said Sarah with comic joy, a grin lighting up her face as she turned back to me.

Then she came over and sat down beside me. "He's so precocious. Sometimes, I think I've created a monster."

There was a pause as she watched me gobble my pancakes. Then I thought of a question I knew I had to ask sometime. "I hope you don't mind me asking, but what happened to his father?"

"No, I don't mind." She said, "It's nice you're asking."

But her face changed—deep sorrow lines suddenly appeared around her mouth and eyes, and she rose immediately and went back to her stove, where she lit a cigarette.

"His father was killed in Viet Nam. He held the same rank in the Green Berets as Michael. I asked Michael if he knew him, but he said he never met him. Michael never talks about Viet Nam. I guess I can't blame him." She let out a long slow column of rising smoke.

"What was his name, Sarah?"

She still had her back to me and I thought perhaps she was crying. She was looking out the window at the mountains, the sky, the earth, the world outside.

"Stuart William Drummond," she said, finally. "He was from up Cripple Creek way. We were married when we were both seventeen, just kids, really. He signed up for his first tour on his birthday."

"I guess Stuart kind of looks like his Dad, huh?"

"Yes, he does," she said, sadness playing in her voice. She was still staring out the window, smoking; then, abruptly, she snubbed out the cigarette and returned to the chores of cleaning up her cooking, her body twitching with agitation. I knew enough to change the subject.

"He's certainly going to break a lot of hearts when he grows up," I said. "He already looks like a buckaroo who just stepped off the rodeo circuit."

That made her smile, and she turned back to me with that glorious grin in full bloom. She was so striking that I about fell off my chair. I could feel my heart beat increasing.

"You shook him up pretty good in the canyon yesterday...by beating Michael, I mean. He's always thought of him as invincible."

"He's confused. I can tell," I said, "But then again, so am I...I'm a little confused myself this morning."

"Don't be, Paul. There's nothing to be confused about."

Heavy footsteps went up the stairs and a moment later, the shower came on.

"I guess so..." I said, my voice trailing off as I returned to eating. "But I'm still confused."

The sweet smell of pot preceded Michael into the kitchen.

"Good day, my friends. How are you all doing on this glorious morning?" He took a pull off his joint, and shook his wet hair from side-to-side: a shaggy magnificence.

His face was bluish in places and a cut traced his lower eyelid. However, he didn't seem to be in any pain.

"Good morning," I said, "how's your face? I'm sorry about the eye. I was aiming for the jaw, but you lowered your head."

Michael barked a short laugh, sat down, and leaned far back on his chair. I took the joint from him, and smoked. Sarah went to the range and poured out four perfectly round and matching circles of batter on the griddle. Her precision was impressive.

We had been on a binge for about a week and had totally neglected our business. Michael and I had a gem company going for about a year. We dealt in a variety of stones, but mostly turquoise. Bracelets, rings, and unset cabs were our staple. I did the stone cutting and setting, while Michael took care of sales and business. Well, most of the time he did.

We would go south to Albuquerque, buy gems from an assortment of mine representatives, then take them back north and sell them all over the Rocky Mountain region. The black case of the gemstone salesman is a common sight in the towns of the west.

About one month ago, we had made a buy off a dealer named Greg Rule. He had some very fine cut and polished turquoise from the Number 8 mine and offered them at a very nice price. Number 8 was the finest turquoise America ever produced. But it's closed now so the stones are rare. There was a catch in the deal, however. It also included three hundred dollars worth of heishi, which we had never bought before. Heishi is a soft stone used mainly to make Navajo roll-type necklaces.

We couldn't really judge the heishi, but we both wanted the turquoise, so we went for the deal at two thousand bucks. Now, after easily selling the turquoise for a nice profit, we were stuck with a pile of low-grade heishi.

Sarah brought him his pancake breakfast and he began to eat.

"It's only noon," I said to Michael. "After you eat, we should go up and see if Miss Moffat wants any of that heishi for her necklaces. She definitely wants more turquoise bracelets. I'm broke, and I figure you must be too." I put the roach in the ashtray.

"What are we going to do if she doesn't want the heishi? We can't just let it sit there on your bench."

I had a vision of the striped, muddy stone in a pile on my workbench.

"I know, Michael, but I can't do anything with it. It has absolutely no grain, just crumbles and falls into the saw."

His face reddened, and I could tell he was raging because he thought he had been beaten in the deal.

"Well then, we'll just pack it up and send it to that store in D.C. They said they'd take anything from us."

"The only reason they said that was because we've been sending them great turquoise." I replied. "If we send them that crap, they'll never buy anything from us again. It'll burn them down as a buyer, do you want that?"

"What are you trying to do? Get a job as my conscience?"

"I'm just giving you the facts. But it is good to hear you realize you don't have a conscience."

"All right, all right; then we'll take it back to Rule. I'm not going to get beat by that little weasel."

With Michael, there was always such fury in the simplest discussion. His eyes flared, and his voice rose all over his sentences, like he was suddenly reliving some ancient challenge. Some fight in the past that would never leave him. And so now, once again, I had become his stand-in adversary. I was used to it and it didn't really faze me anymore. In fact, it kind of amused me.

"How are we going to take it back to Rule?" I asked. "He travels around the west even more than we do."

"I don't know. But we will find him, and when we do, he will take that crap back because it is not all what he said it was."

Each of my questions had their effect on Michael, I could tell, because for a beat, his narration lost coherence. He loved to engage in any battle or combat, even if it was only morning breakfast business chatter.

"It was a package deal," I offered softly. "And the turquoise was fine. Do you really think you have a case?"

"Even if it was a package deal," he thundered, "it was a low deal, and a bad deal, and one which I will not stand for!"

"We still owe him seventy dollars, so we're not getting beat as badly as we might have been."

"That's it, then!"

Stuart came in at that moment and Michael rose from the table and turned away into one of his patented, solitary, and self-congratulatory soliloquies.

"When Rule comes looking for his money, which you know he will, that will be our chance!"

Then, seemingly for Stuart's benefit, Michael spun dramatically back to the table. "Then, and only then, will I settle our disagreement with Mr. Greg Rule. And you can bet it will be done my way!"

At this Michael pulled himself up into his rather diminutive full height, and in an instant his entire aspect softened and changed. Now it was all soft and sweet, if overly dramatic, speech- making.

"But enough of that. Today we must, with all due haste, journey up to that darling, wonderful, but most importantly, that generous old crone, Miss Moffat, who hovers above our little valley in her lofty perch like an American eagle. And we must then sell her things!" He pounded the table for emphasis. "If not all of the numerous bracelets which we have had for one entire month, and not, as yet, been able to distribute, then as many, many, many, as we can!"

"I've been trying to get you up to Miss Moffat's for weeks," I reminded him.

"Well, today, we'll go!" He climaxed and dropped back down into his seat to wolf down his pancakes.

Sarah had been sitting, watching us both and eating her pancakes, occasionally smiling at Michael's bluster, but she hadn't said one word since Michael had come down from his shower.

Now that enough time had passed since yesterday's fighting, in Michael's mind anyway, he wanted everyone to have forgotten his sins. But women retain memories of struggle much longer than men; they're just wired differently I guess. So now as Michael turned to Sarah, smiling wide and boyish, she rose and headed outside, grabbing the food to feed Strider as she exited. Michael gave me a "Wow! Women?" look—and I got up too.

"Let's go see Miss Moffat," I said. "We have to stop at the shop and pick up the box, so we might as well get going now."

I left the kitchen to find my denim jacket. When I got back, Michael was sitting calmly with his elbows on the table, one hand holding the other in front of his mouth. He was watching Sarah feed Strider through the open window. Stuart was gone.

"She digs you, Paul, you know that, don't you?"

"I don't know anything of the sort, Michael. I don't know what she digs."

"Well, whoever turns her head, I hope it doesn't screw us up as friends."

I didn't know what to say.

Getting no answer, Michael rose quickly and took his huge straw cowboy hat off a dowel by the door and went out.

I followed him and my eyes stung in the morning sun's brightness, so I shaded them with my hand. As we were walking to the jeep, Sarah sauntered up between us, and slung her arms around each of our waists, pulling us both in towards her. Her tiny waist seemed too thin to contain such a vibrant human life.

"Well, when my businessmen are through with business and thick with cash, why don't you come to the roof?" Sarah rented a studio above the Loop

Lounge and spent her days creating batik garments for wealthy women.

"All right," I said, "we'll drink a case of Coors and sweat it out at the same time."

My side was tight against her, and I didn't want her to let go. There was a warming force there that I didn't want to abandon.

Michael had already parted. He was already around the other side of the jeep, pausing, then getting in and starting it up. Had there been one more minute, I would have kissed her. I would have turned to face her and placed my lips on hers and pressed down hard. But I didn't.

She stood there with her heart-shaped mouth open only very slightly, her arm around me loosening its grip and then softly sliding across the full length of my back, touching each muscle as she went. Then she held my arm, then my hand, then finally, she let go completely—a stirring sequence I will never forget.

"Good bye, Paul," She said quietly. I thought I heard a faint mountain echo coming down through the trees.

"Goodbye, Sarah."

And I got in.

Michael lifted off in a blast of gravel that sent Sarah running to avoid being stoned. She raised her fist giving us the finger, but also smiling wide, a very incongruous gesture.

CHAPTER IV

A main street, wide and curving through Manitou like a bow: sunlight on the sidewalk transforms the parking meters into sundials. Tourists move slowly through the trinket and souvenir shops; cowboy hats blooming on children's heads like mushrooms. Just outside town, to the west, the cog railway carries people up the first range of Pikes Peak for a view of Colorado Springs and the high plains. From the summit, seven miles west and up, the town looks like a steer bird on the back of a buffalo.

We managed to do pretty well with old Miss Moffat. She had a good deal of backlogged orders, so she virtually emptied our supply of bracelets.

Miss Moffat is the dowager queen of the whole Pikes Peak area. That includes more than one valley and the entire area has been dominated by her family for as long as anyone can remember, going all the way back to the pioneer folk that actually fought off the tribes and held the land with their feet and hands. They were the ones who started ranches in the best-positioned, windbreak-protected corners of the high foothills or in the most enormous feed glades and county-sized meadows.

Miss Moffat's family were the descendants of these pioneers, an independent, violent bunch. They had large families and many children, a fact that overcame the high mortality rate among the family's daredevil young men.

Miss Moffat herself was a kind of silver-haired cowgirl princess. Tall and still trim in her eighties, she'd clearly been a beauty once and seemed determined to stay looking that way. It was widely known that she would always wear an embroidered cowboy hat in the Memorial Day Parade, her gray tresses loose, and her figure lithe and light in the saddle.

These small town beauty queens are now as scarce as a good, small town rodeo. But at one time every little crossroad with a hardware store had its own queen. And Miss Moffat was then, is now, and forever shall be, the Cowgirl Queen of Manitou Springs, Colorado.

Eventually, however, even Miss Moffat took to calling herself an old maid. She claimed there were no men around who could handle her anymore. It is true that she was still as wily and crisp as any female of any age. So I always enjoyed going up to visit her clapboard castle, this old ten-bedroom monstrosity ranch house sitting high in the foothills overlooking the Garden of the Gods.

The Garden of the Gods is a natural formation lying in the foothills of Pikes Peak, its huge vertical stones stretching up into the sky in groups. It is still considered holy ground by many tribes, but now asphalt roads plough all throughout. Miss Moffat's dark old ranch sat just above this ancient formation, soaking up the high desert sunlight like a black stone.

Inside, air conditioners roared to keep the heat out. Miss Moffat met us at her door in the rhinestone-studded costume of a country and western musical star, and seemed to want us to treat her as if she were. You never knew what to expect from a visit to Miss Moffatt's house.

Her family had been among the first in the Pikes Peak area of Colorado. The Moffats were miners and ranchers and had worked together for well more than a century to keep all the valley water in the family. They did so with great success and owned huge tracts of virgin timberland and whole mountains of molybdenum being mined outside of Leadville near the Continental Divide. They used molybdenum as an alloy to make steel hard and "without it our tanks would not have won WWII," or so Miss Moffat often told us.

Michael put on quite a show in her timber temple. At her core, Miss Moffat was still a debutante who loved to flirt, so when Michael turned on the charm she'd just melt. Later she'd get out her checkbook. I've got to admit Michael was very kind of heart towards her the day we went to see her about the bracelets. He got her talking about her youth climbing the hills looking for boyfriends at scarce ranches, but never finding "one man worth a damn." She could shoot better than any man in the valley, but as each world war came around they never allowed her to sign up to be a soldier in any part of "a shooting army."

She told us about how she used to love to dance. There was an old country record playing in the background. Suddenly Michael sprung up from the couch. He pulled Miss Moffat up too and smoothly waltzed her around her parlor. She got right into it and you could see she had been an excellent dancer when she was young. Michael never failed to surprise me with his secret talents. Resting her chin in the crook of his neck, Miss Moffat's warm smile was golden in the light pouring through the room's giant picture window. She was in heaven as Michael danced her around in the dusty air of her own ancient parlor.

Right then I knew we weren't going home empty handed. Michael even managed to convince her to take some heishi, just to fool around with. She was a good smith herself, so I guess she figured she could set it up, somehow. It was impossible, too, for her to refuse Michael once he turned on his charming persona.

Cash in hand again, Michael drove straight to the liquor store, before we went up to visit Sarah. It was nearly three in the afternoon, but the moon was already up, pale and full, and directly opposite the sun. I was always amazed when I could see the sun and moon at the exact same time.

Sarah's studio was a ramshackle afterthought on the roof of the Loop Lounge. Inside we found her hand painting on silk. A soft breeze rippled the fabric as Sarah's nimble arm and brush worked it. Her eyes narrowed in focus as she drew long, strong, arcs across the material. She finished a bold stroke with a flourish and then paused to inspect her design. Finally she looked up at us.

"Hello boys."

In her other hand, she held a jelly jar of dye and continued her brushwork while we opened some beers and pulled up plastic patio chairs.

The studio was oblong with two tall, narrow windows opposite the door. The view looked out at a stairway of mountainous green range. The rest of her walls were raw bare planks covered with hand-drawn clothes designs and an occasional postcard, map or snapshot. As at the cabin, here all the sills and tables and shelves were filled with plants, ferns and flowers, but their fragrance was overwhelmed by the odor of the batik wax and dyes. Wooden drying racks took up half the room, each upright, holding a length of dyed fabric. Patterns and colors varied, but the lines and fusing of shades were clearly all by the same hand. I liked her work. Michael had told me that Sarah had begun selling about two years ago.

"You have to teach me to batik sometime, Sarah," I said. "I'd like to try it." She was wearing one of her own dresses, a column of emerald silk that clung to her body with static electricity. I shivered a little in the warm mountain air.

"It's really fun and not too difficult," she replied, "but very expensive. I have to send away to New York for the dyes, and only the finest fabric will take them without fading. It really runs into money."

She paused, changing colors and brushes, and sipping on a beer I had opened and passed to her. Her eyes danced with delight as she took it, and there was a grin upon her delicate lips.

"I had to pay to learn," she continued, "so I figure I should be paid to teach. It's only fair."

"Oh, sure, I'd be willing to give you something for it. I could pay you off in precious gems."

She laughed and tossed her loose hair. She went looking for her cigarettes, found them and lit one up. I thought to myself that mandala-shaped buns were reserved for evenings only. Michael got up, grunting crankily, and went outside through the slap-shut screen door.

"What's the matter, Michael? Bored?" asked Sarah loudly while blowing out her first puff.

He didn't answer so she went on talking to me. The intricate piece she was working on seemed to be a loose pants design. An explosion of color at the cuffs led up the legs in exquisite streams. I had the same reaction to it as when I'd examined a perfectly woven Persian carpet—there was so much more happening beneath the surface design.

"What is that going to be?" I asked.

"These are yoga pants."

"What's yoga?"

She laughed.

"It is an Indian discipline that combines breathing, meditation and exercise. I practice it every day."

"Oh, well. I never heard of that." I said, instantly feeling a bit out-classed, but I persevered. "How has your selling been going?"

"Very well, actually, but the sewing bogs me down. I've hired a seamstress now, so that should help. I need to get much more stock on-hand before I can hit the larger markets, like city department stores. Handmade art forms are such a new thing, but they're becoming an in-demand commodity too. And I totally feel certain that yoga is going to become commonplace in America in the coming years."

"Really?"

"Yes. It's great exercise."

Sarah lifted several different yoga designs up and draped them over a frame. Outside the window, I could see Michael throwing handfuls of tiny roof gravel down into the streets below. His movements were jerky, twitching, like a bird feeding. He nearly lost his cowboy hat, blowing across the roof and almost over the side, but he recovered it.

"Paul, will you help me lift this?"

We carried a drying rack to the side of the room and placed it in a slot where the fabric could hang free. We were right next to the roof window and now Michael watched as we secured the frame. Then Sarah began putting her materials away, one by one, methodically, purposefully, and meticulously.

I was examining a finished skirt, a design that had a riot of blooming abstract flowers on its hem when I heard Michael outside doing his best imitation of a dog's bark. It was a running joke with us. Whenever we were up there visiting the roof and the Manitou dogcatcher drove by, we'd both start barking and yelping. Invariably, the woman officer would screech to a halt, get her lasso pole out, and hunch over in readiness, patrolling the surrounding streets for ten minutes. I'm certain she felt outwitted by hounds.

"Michael, did you pick up that package for me?" Sarah was facing the sink and her lilting voice was perhaps too low to be heard outside. But for me, it attracted my attention like a whisper—a whisper as soft and delicate as any of her batik designs swaying on their wooden frames.

"What did you say?" Michael called from outside. He was facing the street, looking down at the dogcatcher.

"Did you pick up my package of dyes at the post office? I asked you to, three days ago." Her voice hadn't risen.

He turned towards the studio. "Will you please fucking speak up, Sarah? You know I hate it when you speak so low."

"She asked if you got her package at the post office," I called out loud enough to make certain he would hear.

Michael slammed the screen door hard closing it.

"What are you, her interpreter?" he snarled.

Sarah turned from putting her things away, and looked at him.

"At least Paul cares enough to listen!" she said, her green eyes burning into him.

Michael turned to me and gave me a look that said fuck you in about ten languages. For a second he looked like a soldier again, eyes alert, back erect, and head on the swivel, ready for combat, either verbally or physically violent. But then the rage passed. He swigged his beer, crushed the can, threw it across the room directly into the trash barrel and then went to the refrigerator to fetch another.

"No, I didn't get your fucking package," he said with his back to us, his voice dripping with sarcasm. "But I'm sure your guru over there will be glad to run right over and get it for you."

"Sure," I said, putting my beer down. "I'll go get it."

I was out and gone before Michael could turn around, but I heard his curses follow me as I rambled around and down the back stairway. Sarah's soft frankincense fragrance was still floating in my nostrils like a barely remembered dream.

When I got back, Michael was gone. Sarah's eyes were crying red, and the cheeks below them were still damp. As soon as I walked in, she rushed to me, circling my neck with her arms and putting her head on my chest. She held on tight. I swung the package around behind her back.

"Oh Paul, he was awful to me. He called me a whore." She started to cry, sobbing against my chest.

"He said he knows I want you. He said I have a great talent for breaking up. I don't know why I slept with you, except I wanted to." At this phrase, she looked up at me, her green eyes engaging mine, so powerful, so intense. "But we didn't do anything."

"I know, Sarah," I said laughing. "I couldn't have made love at gunpoint last night."

"But that's not what Michael thinks."

It was already dusk outside. The shadow of our embrace slanted away into the room, the casting light from a street lamp outside. We stayed that way a long time. Just holding each other. Feeling the rise and fall of her breasts against me, I was beginning to forget that I was comforting her. Then she looked up at me.

"Well, what do *you* think, Sarah? How exactly do you feel?" Her head dropped back against my chest.

"I like you, Paul. Very much. I really do. But I hate this feeling that I'm hurting you both by feeling this way. And I do care about Michael, but I can't stand it when he treats me like this. He makes me feel worthless." She finally released her grasp of me and turned around. "I'm so confused now. I don't know what to think."

"I don't either," I said, suddenly idled and alone.

The oval-topped refrigerator stood out luminous and white in the settling darkness. I fumbled for the chrome handle, found it, and got us a couple of beers. Sarah didn't want one, so I put hers back.

"Where is he now?" I said at last. "Did he say where he was going?"

She lit another cigarette.

"No, he just left here cursing me, and trying to kick the stairs down on the way out."

"Well, damn. I don't give a rat's ass what he thinks when he gets like that."

"Oh, Paul, I'm so sorry." She came up to me again, standing right in front of me, with her raised head barely reaching my chin, her scent, her body, her essence. She was just too close not to hold and kiss. I was very conscious of it being our first kiss. It was long, soft, deep, and yet filled with trepidation—all at the same time—a maelstrom of passionate emotions. But when we parted, we parted totally, letting go, and separating completely.

"Listen, Sarah, he is right about one thing. I do like you too, and if this is the way he thinks he can treat you, then he doesn't deserve you."

I cradled her crying face in my two hands. "Listen, look at me. You are perfect, a child of nature, a creature of kindness and pure heart."

She smiled up at me and I went on. "Come on, I'll take you home, then head home myself. Mike's probably there already, since I had the jeep, which reminds me, here's your package."

As I handed it to her, her expression changed. It became more solid, the puffiness of crying suddenly fell away, and for a second, as she turned, I thought I saw a small smile. It didn't seem to have anything to do with my comforting her. Briefly, I had the sensation of entering an enclosure. It passed just as suddenly as it had come.

She placed the package on her bench, shut the lights, and I followed her out. It was a clear night. We both paused on the roof to take it in.

Once down in the jeep, it only took a moment to reach Sarah's house. Other than a quick goodbye, neither of us had anything to say for the trip.

During the night, a dream: a flash-flood storm washes out a stripe down the mountain slope like a newly cut power line. Boulders house-high carry out into the valley below for half a mile. A creek and pass are born.

CHAPTER V

A log cabin, built crudely square with its back close up against a high wall of cracked granular sandstone. Inside the cabin, the timber rafter beams are exposed, some still retaining spots of hundred year-old bark. The floors are not plumb and creak loudly under any weight, but are worn shiny smooth from decades of booted feet. An oversized cable spool lying on its side serves as the room's only table, and except for a rocker and a stuffing-leaking sofa, the main room is entirely bare of furniture. The A-frame loft above is low, and encourages people sitting on the couch to use caution rising. The cabin's main door faces the red stonewall outside, but the kitchen windows opposite look down and across town, unobstructed for miles.

Voices woke me up. Our cabin has strange acoustics. No matter where you are, it always seems like everyone is speaking around a small table.

Rolling over, I was surprised to see it was still dark out. In between the logs, which were the loft floor, I could make out three figures on the couch chattering like crows. Intermittently, there was the sound of someone tapping rapidly on glass. The first creaks of my waking quieted them, but in a few minutes, they were even louder than before. With Michael in the lead reciting another poem, I gave in and got up.

"Good morning, Paul!" called Michael. "Come on down, I've got something for you."

The stairs down were flat split logs at irregular intervals. About halfway down, I recognized our guests. The shorter one, Joe O'Choate, was a dark guy whose face was swallowed by glasses and unrestrained black hair. He was an easterner, and I think, a tree surgeon. The other guy was Miss Moffat's nephew. Roger Moffat was the single male scion of that wealthy old family who had inherited a huge piece of land about fifteen miles in towards Cripple Creek. I heard he was a black sheep, professional gambler, and that he kept a string of fighting cocks out there. Miss Moffat never spoke of him. Neither of them knew me.

"Hey," I greeted them.

"Good morning, Paul. This is Joe and Roger," said Michael. As they looked at me, I noticed that all their eyes were interchangeable, red lids half-closed and tender as sunburn.

"Good morning, fellas."

Although it was cold on this mountain morning, the hearth was bare so clouds of condensation hung about our heads like comic character balloons. I grabbed some birch bark and set about building a fire.

"Never mind with that, Paul. Look what we've got," said Michael. He held up a small, white packet, keenly folded and about half the size of a wallet photo: cocaine.

If I frowned, they didn't notice. For the first time, I saw the mirror and the razor blade on the table before them. The razor looked very sharp.

"You do coke, don't you?" asked O'Choate. "I mean everybody does coke!"

"I never met anyone who turned it down," added Moffat, dryly.

Michael held up the packet for the entire time I built the fire. His grin was tilted, like the col between two peaks of different heights. He was delighted with himself. Probably most of the money that Michael and I had made selling bracelets the day before was in that tight, white envelope.

But I held my tongue.

Yelling at Michael wasn't going to make anything better. He was operating on powdered sleep, so for him, until the coke ran out, all was right with the world.

We had done coke together before, especially when we first met. But we found it didn't go well with business. We were both so undisciplined that we would spend all our profits on the next score, not to mention how much more we drank to relax.

"It's uncut, Paul. We went all the way to Pueblo to get it. I'll put out a line for you." Michael carefully opened the packet, and using the razor as a scoop, he put some of the sparkling white powder on the mirror before him. Meticulously, he began to crack and further pulverize.

"I don't think I want any."

All three of them looked up at me, stunned.

O'Choate and Moffat even allowed a grin. They were glad. It meant more for them. They both lit cigarettes and quickly hot-boxed them.

"The first and foremost affect of doing cocaine is the desire to do more cocaine." I meant it. Coke is a bottomless pit where you wind up with no money, no friends, and no life.

"I'd rather eat. I'm starved. Besides, what the hell time is it? Six o'clock in the morning? You guys are insane."

Michael immediately went back to tapping out the coke. With three dramatic arm swoops he laid out three white lines curving across the surface of the mirror. Using a twenty-dollar bill, rolled up into a tube, he leaned over and running quickly along the first line drew half the coke into his right nostril. He paused as the drug hit his brain. He smiled. Then he quickly repeated this process with his other half. The other two did theirs in their own particular style.

"I can't believe you don't want any, Paul. But I understand; I'll save some for you." Michael's eyes were wide open and his face muscles moved slowly into a reptilian smile.

"Yeah, save it for me." I said.

O'Choate was sniffling and poking his nose. I noticed that all three were now sitting on the edge of the sofa.

"Can we put some music on now?" asked O'Choate. He rose and went over to my receiver. Switching it on, the room filled suddenly with blaring rock. As O'Choate danced his way back to the couch, he directed a question to Rob. "So when's the big party, Rob? You've been talking about it for weeks."

"Soon, real soon," said Moffat.

"Did you hear, Paul? Rob is having a party out at his ranch," said Michael.

"What kind of party?" I may have lacked enthusiasm.

"A big party," said Moffat.

"With cockfights, Paul. Can you believe it? Cockfights! I haven't been to a cockfight since 'Nam.

For Christ's sake, I've been living in this valley for two years and all the damn time, this crazy fucker has been staging cockfights fifteen miles outside of town."

"And betting on them, don't forget that," O'Choate said, "and betting on them."

"What's a cockfight without gambling?" asked Moffat.

"Have you ever been to a match, Paul?" asked Michael.

"In Mexico," I said. "When is this party?"

"Next week."

"How many fights will there be?" I asked. I'd also been to a few matches in Arizona and New Mexico. It was an underground circuit, but I'd met some of the players.

"Probably ten," answered Moffat. "Birds from all over are coming. I own three."

"I bet one of them is a ringer," I said with no inflection. Moffat stopped his bobbing around instantly, now examining me with greater detail.

"All my birds are game," he said.

I could see Michael was enjoying this. He loved any kind of conflict.

"Well, when is it?" asked O'Choate. "I mean, what day?"

"Next week," said Moffat, still looking at me.

I left them to get some breakfast.

The kitchen was even colder. You really can't live in the mountains unless you like to build fires. Even in the height of summer it is still a daily chore. In winter, it's your main activity.

City people build big fires, pyres, really, like they had to consume something. But here, you didn't want to waste the wood. Heat comes in direct proportion to the amount of energy you expend in gathering it. I built little fires.

It generally took at least eleven cords of seasoned wood to get through a winter in our cabin. That's a pile six feet high all the way around our little log chalet. We ran short two years ago and I promise you, that was never ever going to happen again.

After breakfast, I went outside and around to where the cabin roof eaved over our woodpile. Finding the sledge and wedges tucked amidst the timber, I went to the edge of our bluff where big tree trunk sections of wood stood waiting to be split. After taking off my flannel shirt I started to split wood.

Our wedges were old, their edges bent over into uneven chipped ends. Once I hit a wedge so hard that I heard the metal piece fly by my ear like a high-speed mosquito.

Another time, Michael passed by just as another wedge chip took off buzzing like a bullet. Michael hit the ground instantly. Then he just stood up and walked away without saying a word.

He was always on alert, on the swivel, they called it in the army. I'd actually seen him turning his head back and forth looking for trouble when we'd enter a new bar, or when we'd be driving up some tricky mountain road. His eyes were always alert and looking for peril. Training from Viet Nam, I guess. I asked him about it, but he never answered. Actually, he never mentioned Viet Nam at all, or anything that happened to him there. I know, because I'd asked him. He'd clammed right up.

Splitting wood on your own takes a good, long while, with lots of pauses to rest between hardbound labors. Sometimes, I'd bury a wedge in a tree chunk without splitting it. Then sink in another whole wedge before the trunk would finally give way, and part. It was a small success as each piece fell.

Later, stoking the fire, I'd use a piece that I remembered splitting. I'd sit there, warm and relaxed, remembering the work I'd done on a day months before.

Crude cabins covered the slopes all around me. We were high on the first range, which gave us privacy, but if I looked directly down the mountain there was a spread right beneath us. The house was elaborately planked and had two stories. It was built in the thirties by a millionaire who employed half the valley building it. The house and the grounds had gone to seed over the years, and had become ramshackle.

As I rested, leaning on the sledge handle, a boy came out from this tumbledown house far below. The sound of the screen door slamming reached me a few seconds after I'd seen it shut. It was that far away.

The boy was carrying a fishing pole, and headed straight for a swimming pool. The pool was square and fringed with a green scum. I'd never seen anyone swimming in it. Without any hesitation, the lad set a lawn chair on the edge, baited his hook, and dropped in his line.

In a few moments, he had his first strike. Calmly, after a short battle, with his fishing line drawing ripple graphs in the pool, he reeled in a fish. In fifteen minutes, he had three good-sized trout, and carrying them, he went back into the house for breakfast.

Another fifteen minutes was enough for me, too. Six tree trunks now sectioned and split and another few days of heat for next winter. I stacked them below the kitchen window, and went around. The red cliffs outside our door changed color as low clouds passed overhead. At one time, there had been a waterfall here, part of a creek that ran past the cabin, but it was long dry now.

Sandstone is tough to climb on. It crumbles easily, and won't take a piton. Michael and I had explored the plateau at the top when we first moved in, but I hadn't been up there for ages. It's strange, but I liked the idea of having my back to these rocks. The cabin's back, I mean. It's sort of like facing the door in a saloon: impossible to be taken by surprise. Voices carried out to me, so I went inside.

Everyone always looks up when you enter a one-room structure, especially a mountain cabin. The door creaked as I shut it, and they went back to talking.

As I was going upstairs for my climbing tools, Michael asked, "Want to do some coke now, Paul?"

"No," I said. "Not now."

CHAPTER VI

A dark mass, suspended by rope, and rappelling down the face of a reversed cliff: coming in and out of sight, like a squirrel circling a tree. Blackness backs most other objects. The only light is a fusing of pastels along the western horizon. The lowest hue is a light green, seemingly drawn out of the conifer trees it hovers above. The last range prisms this light off in beams, a hundred signal mirrors. Below, in Colorado Springs, streetlights come on in marching rows. Headlight pairs sniff along the highway, its traffic eased by dusk. On the red cliff face, a climber's long, umbilical rope chafes the granular stone over several points. But his descent does not vary, he drops in pace with the sun.

Off-belay, I thought to myself as my toes touched the ground. My rope led up and away from me, like a snake charmer's; releasing the bitter end, I watched as it sped up to the last piton, through it, and fell back down to me.

I am the climb. When I'm scaling this cliff it's like my hands adhere to that sandy stone and for a few minutes the precipice and I are one. Gripping minute ridges you can barely see, using just my fingertips, I pull myself up inch-by-inch.

Sometimes I over-extend myself and wind up trapped under an overhang some place half way up, sweating scared. But then I just go for the reach anyway, and I usually complete the move.

But I have fallen. Tumbled free-fall for about twenty feet once, until the safety line reached my last hammered piton and broke my fall; a completely gut-wrenching experience that shows I should probably always climb with a partner.

But here, alone in the dusk of this nameless mountain, I feel completely myself. Pressing my fingers into the cracks and crevices of this rock face makes me feel like this mountain belongs to me, and I to it. Like I am reaching directly into Colorado's guts to haul myself up.

And every time I complete this same anonymous ascent, it's a totally unique, solitary and gripping achievement. Once again I know exactly what I can and cannot do, and who I am.

I am at my best on this mountain and I hope to climb it as long as I am alive.

My hands were stiff and scraped from the sandy stone descent. While coiling my climbing rope, I felt good: spidery, and pleasantly exhausted, but also self-satisfied after a good hard day of coordinated, often perilous exertion.

By the time I reached the cabin door, night had sealed up around me like a bottle. As it creaked open, I could see two figures in the dimness, their movements distributing jittery shadows around the room like a calliope.

"Oh, hello, Paul!" It was Shake, a stone buyer who looked particularly glad to see me. "Michael didn't say you were around."

He shook my hand hard and slapped me on the back, moving me away from Michael towards the warmth of the fire inside.

"Gee, you look flushed...your face, I mean. It couldn't be that cold out there. I mean I haven't been here that long, have I?" He turned to Michael for a second, then back to me. He wore rimless glasses that reflected the yellow lantern light. Trails of sweat ran down both sides of his face. His hair was short, and looked as if he'd cut it himself without the aid of a mirror. Despite all this, or maybe because of it, I liked him. He was a good client who had made a mistake.

"Shake, we're talking business," said Michael, still in the half-light. "Now you owe me four hundred dollars. And you've owed me that for more than a year, a year and a..."

"Us, Michael. He owes us," I corrected. My pack of gear made a clinking thud as the metal pitons inside hit the floor. For a moment, I ignored both of them as I squatted down to warm my hands and chest by the fire.

"Alright, he owes us," Michael continued in a huff, "but he hasn't paid us."

Shake took up a position of safety directly behind me where Michael couldn't get at him. After a second's pause, while he checked to see if Michael would attack, he turned to me to explain.

"That's what I came here for, Paul. To tell you guys I'd have half what I owe you the day after tomorrow. I got a job welding, and Thursday is payday."

For the first time, Michael came completely out of the darkness and I could see his face. It was red and bagged with sleeplessness.

"Half? What the hell good is half?" he screeched, his flinty eyes darting around the cabin haphazardly. "You got your goods. They were some of the most beautiful opals I'd ever seen. From Queretaro,

Mexico, $33.60 a carat. I remember. And that was a special price because we were doing it for a friend."

Michael paced beside the staircase.

"What the hell good is half?" he said, again.

I ignored him, and spoke softly to Shake. "Half sounds good, Shake. Relax, it sounds fine."

Shake sat down quickly on the couch at that, perched on its edge.

"Well, Michael doesn't seem to think so," he went on. "I've been trying to convince him for an hour, and he's just gotten madder and madder. And there's just no way I can get the money sooner. But it's a good job, and I can pay the rest off in a couple of weeks. I mean I'm making good money."

"But you've owed us for over a year," said Michael, the muscles in his neck tightening visibly. Then he closed in on Shake again who popped up to avoid contact. He actually got around Michael by hopping over the arm of the couch. He looked like a kitten escaping a curious dog. I had to laugh.

"Will you relax, Michael?" I said, "Shake says he'll have half the cash Thursday. You can have that first half, and I'll wait for mine." Shake relaxed, visibly. He hadn't expected this. Michael closed in on me.

"You know what you are, Paul? You're just stupid." He was only a few inches away from me, and his breath stank of sour whiskey. My attention wavered, and for a moment, I had visions of Michael's beard as a replanted forest. It was hard to keep from smiling. Right around then, I decided to move down to the store for a while. Michael was still talking at me.

"I do every goddamned thing I can to get a decent business on its feet, and I make one mistake: you. And the whole thing just falls apart." He turned away into another self-centered soliloquy.

"I do the buying, the selling, and you can't even collect a bad debt. All you can do is chop up good stones into piles of waste and crap. I don't know how I got into this partnership."

Watching Shake's face, also listening, I realized he was taking Michael seriously. Our business reputation was just now bearing the fruits of work I had done last summer, and the summer before that. We now actually had good, steady, paying customers. If they heard about a breach between us as partners, even one silly internal rift like this might make an impression and turn them off. And Shake was a total gossip. In any case, I wanted Shake out of there so I could get to bed.

"Come on Shake, let's go outside." With my hand on his shoulder, I turned him away from Michael, who had his back to us, still ranting and raving. With me guiding him out Shake and I exited the dark cabin into the darker evening.

The sky was now muted full with gray black-bottomed clouds. Their thickness gave them a puffy texture, and directly overhead, the appearance of being the joint of a great seashell. We couldn't see any stars. Shake's car was parked down the road apiece, just before the last, steepest incline. I walked along with him, concerned with his impression.

"How's your job?" I asked.

"Good. Real good. I think I'll be welding a long time. Oh no, not really. But it is a fine cash source. It's not my career, but how many career welders are there?"

"Lots. Alaska's full of them. A good welder up there can make sixty grand."

"No shit. Where'd you hear that?" He seemed genuinely interested. I felt a small success.

"From a welder I know. He went up there and worked for the oil companies. Made a killing and came back and bought a horse ranch on the southern plateau."

"Well then he's not a career man."

"No, I guess you're right. But it is a valuable skill."

The cloud shell sky hinged open as we walked along and the stars came out. Shake's car was stuck off the road on the dirt shoulder. We stopped beside it. Suddenly Shake became very conspiratorial.

"Paul, I heard about some uncut gemstones around. They're looking for a cutter. Do you want me to mention your name?" He smiled, looking back up the hill, "I know you can cut."

"Sure," I said, "I'll be staying down at the store for a while. I can always use freelance work—maybe more so now!"

We both laughed, and he got in. Until it started up, I had forgotten about his Chevy's lack of a muffler. He swung the car around in a circle and headed down, beeping. Even after he was out of sight, I could still hear his car, the roar dull, then sharp, as it ricocheted around the notch.

Chapter VII

A cabin loft: sparsely furnished with its low ceiling lit only by a gas-powered camping lantern. The small single window alternately rattles in the wind, then falls silent. Within the lantern light, a young man is moving about folding up his clothes and packing an old, large, wicker steamer trunk. His gas lantern-thrown shadow looms large behind him, casting sharp-edged shadows upon the log walls like a kabuki show. Below him on the near main floor, a man sleeps noisily on an ancient sofa. As the young man continues packing he notices what appears to be a large military journal on a low side table beside the single weary mattress. It's a volume he has never seen before anywhere in the cabin, and certainly not on this table: it is old, and olive-drab army-style. Its weathered and water-stained cover

*is completely bare of any text, but upon opening it,
the man reads the faded cover page:*

```
United States Army - Special Forces
Officer: Michael Boyd Atman
Combat Journal
First Entry: 1/12/65 Base: Cam Ranh Bay, SVN
Last Entry: 11/12/68 Base: Sapporo, Japan
```

*Sitting down, he leans back against the open chest
and pulls the hissing lantern closer. Breathing in
deeply, he begins to read.*

Michael had been asleep for hours when I found it. It was made of some man-made material that seemed indestructible. Even the pages were treated with something to make them waterproof. There was a pen attached by a string with a special pouch in the binding to store it. It had taken a lot of abuse, but it seemed like that's what it was designed to do. Even so, I found myself handling it very gingerly.

I had never even seen it before, but I knew right away what it was. It was his Army journal. At that moment it never occurred to me that Michael would mind if I read it.

The first entries were about arriving in country: Viet Nam, his impressions of the landscape and climate, of the officers and men he met and liked. Then he started getting into action—a lot of firefights, an entry where he described an ambush where he was wounded. I read another where his unit was nearly captured while patrolling a VC stronghold.

I read for quite a while before I realized who his brother officer was. Who his partner was. He called him "Capt. D," for short most of the time, but once in a while he got chatty and called him "Stu." Then, a little later, "that bum, Drummond!"

Captain Stuart Drummond was Michael's partner. It had to be the same Drummond. It had to be Sarah's husband. Skimming the next couple of entries, he wasn't mentioned again. So I skipped to the closing entry, and here, just as I found it, is what I read:

Nov. 12 '68

--It's been a long time since I've written here. Big gap! Things slowed WAY down after that last entry. We hadsecured the countryside completely so there wasn't much to document. Then something big happened.

But I had to tell about it so many times and in so many places and to so many people that I didn't feel like writing it down, but now I do.

I'm in Japan now, Sapporo. Been out of Nam since August. Haven't had a rifle in my hands in four months. In three weeks,

I stand down to the states. A week later, home. Colorado.

I've been going through frickin' endless debriefings and examinations. First ones were more like hearings, except they were barred to the press. Good Goddamn thing too. Those were the very early ones, the ones in Saigon. Army didn't bring charges against me; once my story checked out, they threw a blanket over the whole affair and destroyed the paperwork. It wouldn't have been good for morale.

I was cleared, but I was discharged: Distinguished Service. For Christ's sake, I was there almost five years, I was getting used to the jungle.

The only thing that really bothers me is Mrs. Drummond, the wife. Stu used to tell me about her. I've got her picture right here. I asked for Stu's gear and they gave it to me. I feel real bad about Mrs. Drummond. I mean she wasn't involved, but she's the most affected. And he had a son, too. I mean, she still does. Stuart, named after his dad.

I have weird thoughts about my place in all this, my responsibility. The thoughts don't bother me as much as the weirdness in my own head that accompanies them.

That's why I have to write it all down now, here. While I still have it fresh

*in my mind. The way it actually happened
to me.*

*So, it was last spring in Cambodia—I'm
not supposed to say that. I'm supposed
to say Viet Nam, but what's the difference? The difference is it's the truth,
and I'm going to tell the truth here.
It was dust and mud season and the only
thing that made it bearable were the cool
nights. Every morning, I would get up
and think Jeez, another day toward home.
Some days, it just didn't ring true.*

*Where we camped, they had long ago
defoliated. Our camp was a huge empty
circle in a bare forest. A clearing of
a bunch of concentric circles defending
the perimeter. The killing area was the
first, largest zone, the first two hundred yards inside the bush. Several runs
of barbed wire, claymores, mines, bunkers, and foxholes made up this initial
line of defense, our first berm.*

*The next line was the inner circle,
where all our buildings were. There was
a hardstand and a chopper pad. The inner
circle is much smaller, but is ten feet
higher, fortified with walls of sand-
bags. They call this kind of base a FOFB—
Forward Observer Fire Base.*

*Ours was small compared with most,
with only fifty troops, all Montagnard
Indians, who spent as much time in the
bush as inside the wire, so our troop*

size didn't really say much about our position strength. Also, we liked to think
we were immediately re-enforceable, but
who knows what the truth was.

Together with Lieutenant Drummond, I
had commanded this unit for two and a
half years. We were both Green Berets.

When we first arrived in the Cambodian
mountains, there were twelve of us, a
full contingent. We treatied with those
Indians and set up the unit. Then we
armed them to the teeth, trained them
to be even better soldiers than they already were, and sent them out looking for
trouble.

There hadn't been any action in the
area before, but we knew the Viet Cong
supply lines were somewhere nearby.

Using VC techniques, we assaulted
the enemy. We marched for days and attacked. We set up trailside claymores. We
laid crossfire ambushes. Bought inform-
ers. Destroyed VC sympathetic villages.
Burned crops. We fought the Goddamn Viet
Cong wherever we found them. Sometimes
fighting went on for days. Sometimes
very close, and dangerous. Knife fights.
Hand-to-hand combat. Everything. God.

Finally, I got wounded. Everybody got
wounded. Those Indians were brave and
they loved to fight. They fought better
wounded. They taught me more about the
jungle, how to move around silently in

it, than all the damn drill sergeants
back at Fort Bragg put together into one
big gaping, frickin' ape.

By last spring, things had been quiet for a long while. USAF over-flight
confirmed that no North Vietnamese Army
(NVA) had been observed in our sector for
over two months. And those fly guys had
infrared cameras to see the red balls at
night, so I guess it was really true. No
one was out on those trails. HQ told us
our sector was SECURED.

For a long while, all I did was smell
the mornings, and walk patrols. Counting
the days toward home.

For my partner, things didn't go so
well. Started with him coming in from a
patrol one day. One of his flank men had
triggered a grenade booby trap that would
have killed him—Drummond—as the slack
man in the patrol line. But it didn't go
off. The trip vine was too old and loose
to blow the explosive. But it was sure
Goddamn enough to upset Drummond, though.
He came back completely freaked out.

I couldn't believe his initial reaction to me. I couldn't believe what he
told me. I remember it exactly because it
really shook me up. I mean here was this
amulet wearing, gook killing old hand
telling me, and I quote, about Charlie—

He told me you don't go into the bush
for a while, and Charlie's still right

there waiting for you, silent as the
fucking tomb. So you go back in, and if
you're not tuned up, you're not ready,
then he'll gore your guts out. He'll kill
you. But if you chicken out, if you don't
go back out there into that swamp then
you'll gore your own guts out.

For Christ's sake's, as if I hadn't
heard that before. As if every soldier
in Viet Nam hadn't heard something like
that that from some grunt before or something just as stupid and obvious.

I knew Drummond had said it to himself to calm himself down. To comfort his
fears and all that. Remind himself of
the importance of being awake and aware.
I also knew that his little speech was
just an admonishing finger within his own
brain pointing back toward common sense,
even though common sense had nothing to
do with surviving where we were. I had
thought Drummond was way past getting
the shivers like that.

It was the first sign of trouble,
meaning I probably should have reported
in to HQ sooner and in more detail about
how he was acting. But I didn't and I
regret that now.

But I did talk to Drummond. I talked
to him everyday. I told him he was getting spooky. But he was quickly beyond
warnings. He was spooky and he knew it
already. It wasn't ignorance that had

him. It was pure fear, like I had never seen. Stuart was scared.

It all came to a head with the problem of the weapons. We hadn't had fire contact in eleven weeks, and the troops were pretty restless. They wanted to return to their own villages. They all lived seventy, maybe couple hundred klics away, in the mountains along the border. The only problem was, they wanted to keep their weapons. Right. American Army weapons that Drummond and I issued them. Weapons that we were responsible for. Weapons that would probably—eventually—wind up in NVA hands if we let them go.

And an M-16 was worth a lot more than just money on the black market to an Indian mountain man. It could mean protection for his entire family for a year. They all had their own weapons anyway, so ours were expendable. Tradable, a luxury item that could be exchanged for something good. It was a lousy problem for us soldiers. It didn't happen often, but it happened. Sometimes you could get the weapons back, and sometimes you couldn't. You could never get them all back.

I was shaving when Drummond came in to see me on the morning of the incident. He didn't sit down, but rather hovered around me as I was shaving, continually trying to look me in the eye through the mirror.

He told me the situation had come to maturity, something military-crazy like that.

I asked him what he meant, and he said that that night the troops informed him of a final meeting to quote 'say farewell.' Then they were going. Taking everything with them, guns, ammo, explosives, everything

He spit that information out like the seeds of a watermelon. We were in government-issue jungle gear, were both sweating, but he was sweating heavily. I tried to joke with him. Calm him down. Show him the big picture. Our mission was already a success. The area was safe. We had done our job. But he wouldn't listen.

He kept talking about how we issued those materials, and were responsible for them. No way was he going to let them leave armed.

I told him to relax. Orders were to do our best. It'd work itself out. He flat out told me no. I remember I stopped shaving and just looked at him, eye-to-eye. We stood there silent and he started twitching under my stare. Then I casually asked him about our patrols to let him off easy. I out ranked him, which he knew.

Finally he said that patrols were in the field as usual, that everything was accounted for. The men hadn't laid down on their duties yet. I asked him what time the meeting was; it was an hour after sunset, about 21:30.

I said I'd call in and let HQ know what was happening. After that, I'd check the western quadrants and that would take me right up to meeting time. He seemed okay with that. Watched me finish shaving and then looked like he was going to leave. I can still taste the dull soapy film of the shaving cream on my tongue even now. It was a day I wish I hadn't lived through. I stopped him leaving, and told him I hated to slap him back, but that all decisions were mine. He knew that. I knew he did. And then he left.

I knew right then I needed to cover my ass so I made my way down to the radio bunker. This was the smartest thing I did. I raised HQ and spoke with the CO on duty, Captain Jules Rene Bakt, an old Special Forces hand who had been in Indo China since the French. I filled him in on the probable breakup of our unit. He wasn't surprised. You cannot keep these native units together without action. He asked me about the weapons, and I laid it all out. He told me what I expected. He said do the best you can with the bastards and that he'd have a chopper standing by.

It was high noon hot when I left the radio bunker. I was on duty for a daytime sweep and I remember being pissed off about that. It was going to be a bad day for a walk in the sun. I really wasn't even thinking about the evening meeting, or about where I might wind up next if our unit did break up. All the stuff you think I'd have been thinking about I didn't. Just picked up my weapon and headed out to the western perimeter to meet my patrol team.

It took nearly the whole afternoon to sweep that empty quadrant. A lot of bonin' around and lookin', but we didn't see any sign that anybody had been moving through there except us. One thing did happen though.

On the way back in, just before we hit the perimeter, the point man stopped us with hand signals. Then he signaled me up, and the flanks in. When I got there, he was squatting against the trunk of a tree taking advantage of what little shade the bare branches provided. The other men sat around him leaving a space across from him that was for me. His name was Cao-Ly, one of the best point men I've ever worked with, and one of our chief scouts.

He asked if they could talk with me. He was very formal about it, since he had been schooled by the French, and spoke English with French grammar. Of course I said yes.

He asked if I had been told that many were returning to the mountains that night, to their homes. I could tell he had worked out his speech beforehand.

He said that for a long time there had been no enemy to fight there. Before that, they fought hard for a long time, so they had to go now, so there wouldn't be any more fighting.

He said there were other places they could go to fight, but that first, they had to go home for a while.

I told Cao-Ly I understood, and that Lieutenant Drummond had informed me and I respected their desires to go home. Then I said that I knew all of them, and we had fought together closely for a long time. That we were friends who had bled together and this was a bond beyond all others, but there was a problem, our weapons. I told him I knew they all had their own weapons besides those we had issued to them. I said, why not leave ours behind? I told him surely he could understand my responsibility. I had to account for these weapons to my superiors.

One of the younger men, an intense, dark fellow whom we nicknamed Dondi because of his youthful appearance, said that the guns were needed at home. And by themselves, so they could get home. Some lived close but some were going to have to walk for many days on dangerous trails to reach their mountains.

I didn't know what to say.

They all exchanged glances with each other, and then looked back to me. Cao-Ly said they had been deeply honored to fight and bleed beside us. So they wished to say that they had talked about this very much among themselves and they were all definitely going, that they were needed where we could not go. In Laos, the Khmer Rouge were striking deeper. They had to go as one unit, so they would be strong. I didn't quite know how to be counted for the record at that point, so I didn't say anything.

Once again, a glance went around the small circle of men and came back to me.

Cao-Ly said that was why they had stopped there on that cooling evening; he said they had stopped for a private parting. He took some steps toward me and touched my shoulder. As he did so, a small necklace dropped from his hand into my lap. One by one, the other men followed. Some mentioned the names of other men not present, some of who were dead, and then, one by one they dropped gifts into my lap. By the time I was alone, it was filled, and I had enough amulets, charms and talismans to keep me safe from danger for centuries.

I wasn't sweating much, there in that weak shade, so I sat alone that way for a long while. Then I got up, gathered up my gifts, bagged them, called the password to the defense perimeter and went back to camp. I went straight to my tent to lie down, and in two minutes, I was asleep.

Drummond woke me up. I guess I slept about two hours. He shook me awake, so I was startled. Grabbing his arms I shoved him back hard, and told him he needed to chill out. Then I sat up, swung my legs over and stood up. The tent was hot and I was still sweating even though the evening had settled. But there was a new fragrance in the tent that I didn't recognize. I tracked it to my pack where my new gifts from the troops were stored. The scent of all my new amulets and charms was heavy and sweet. Drummond really woke me up. He told me they'd all gathered in the inner circle. All of them, and were waiting for us there.

When I lit the lamp I was surprised to find Stuart in full jungle camouflage, strapped with his M-16. I hadn't seen him wear his Green Beret in months, but he had it on now. Perfectly formed, too. By the book. But still pouring sweat, like me. I threw water on my face, pulled on a T-shirt, strapped on my revolver and left the tent. He followed me down between the bunkers till we came up on the inner circle.

Here we found a circle of many, many men, some sitting, some standing, but all turned towards us. I almost smiled to see them all there. They were wearing everything we had ever issued to them: every rifle, pistol and grenade. For a traitorous second I thought to myself that that stuff belonged to them a lot more by blood than it did to Uncle Sam. But duty called me, and the thought passed.

One of the younger men, Sin-Thu, greeted me. For some unknown reason he was called Anh Dung, and he spoke first. He was a brave enough fellow. But I had never gotten to know him. I did remember that Drummond didn't like this guy at all: long standing dislike.

I greeted all the troops present. They could tell I had just woken up because I had heard a joke in their language about what bad karma it is to wake someone up only to tell them goodbye. So I smiled back at them to signal that I too had gotten the little joke. We all smiled. We were a happy bunch again for a moment.

On a subtle signal from Anh Dung, all those standing sat in unison. Now a Captain can always recognize the authority of another Captain. Later, I came to understand that Lieutenant Drummond was already aware of this change in our native leadership. He knew, but hadn't told me, that Anh Dung, a man he hated, was now secretly leading our native force, and he had undoubtedly made the decision to take the long walk home.

I spoke to Anh Dung, addressing him as Captain. I spoke to them in their own intricate language. I could speak it okay, but Drummond understood nothing about it and the sound of it made him nervous, so I was taking a chance, but many of our men laughed, and I thought I saw Cao-Ly smile. I reminded him we had fought together a long time. We had taken good care of each other. I said I could see now, as they were all gathered together on the darkened evening, that they were going, but that also I had to ask if they had to take away all that we had given them, leaving us with nothing but the jungle night.

My speech in their dialect was very well received for its eloquence, I could see that. These grizzled soldiers loved that I could speak to them in their native tongue. But the focus and actual meaning of my message went totally unheeded.

Anh Dung told me that the situation had been discussed before, and that they needed arms where they were going, and also to get there. He repeated what I had said: the jungle night has many eyes and they had many enemies.

Drummond had become agitated, wanting to know what Anh Dung was saying. He demanded to know what they were planning, calling them bastards. And in that second we lost their respect. Drummond's fear was too obvious. Anh Dung had not started out on a par with me, but Drummond's anxiety was a boon for them. Why should they stay with a man who was so afraid? It was over in a second and I knew it.

A murmur of solidarity went around Anh Dung's men. They were now all in agreement and about to depart. Anh Dung picked up his weapon, which had lain beside him, and symbolically he laid it across his own legs, at the ready. The eyes of the entire crowd of soldiers turned back to me.

So, right there, at that moment, as far as I, Michael Boyd Atman was concerned, my duty had been done, fulfilled, over. I had tried to get the weapons back and they had declined. They were going and they were taking the weapons with them. And there was an end to it. They had served me, and Drummond, and Uncle Sam, and the USA quite well, and now they simply wanted to keep the tools of the trade we had given them and go home. So be it. I was about to say so, when I noticed Drummond behind me and to my left. His M-16 was now un-slung, and the barrel was coming up to be level with the crowd. I

*wasn't sure what he was up to, but I went
on. I repeated that Captain Drummond and
I would have nothing to defend ourselves
if they left with everything.*

*One of the Indians yelled out in
English that we should call a chopper and
they all laughed, but Anh Dung scolded
him. Then Anh Dung stood up, keeping his
men seated, and began to walk around.*

*He said he would only say it only one
more time, that there was nothing for
them to do here anymore; So they would
now return home, where they were needed
by their own people. Then on to where we
could not go. Further into Cambodia. As
he spoke, out of the corner of my eye, I
noticed one of his men drop off into the
darkness of the outer circle and disappear. Then another. Drummond was watching Anh Dung, so I didn't think he'd seen
anything.*

*Anh Dung said some of their people
were without defenses because they were
with us. He said that they were soldiers
and had to go home to defend their own
people.*

*I saw more and more men dropping off
and disappearing, and I saw that Drummond
had seen that too and had leveled his
weapon. The air had shifted like some
barometer dropping, and in an instant
everything started to veer out of my control. I knew what was coming but couldn't*

stop it. Anh Dung droned on as two more men dropped off into the jungle, and then Drummond sprung, screaming to them to halt or he would shoot. His voice was just full of hatred. But the departing men didn't stop.

I heard Drummond snap the safety click off on his M-16. It was the worst sound I ever heard. The safety had prevented him from firing. I heard it click off very clearly, but still couldn't believe he'd shoot. I screamed at him what the hell was he doing? I was about twelve feet away.

His first blast killed two men just before they reached the outer balustrades and the safety of the jungle. No one had expected this. Maybe I should have had my gun out, been more ready, but this was just beyond comprehension. He was killing his own men. Our other Montagnard men hit the deck, pinned down under his line of fire. Anh Dung dove for cover in a bunker.

Drummond became robotic. He fired and fired, reloaded quickly and kept firing: pop-pop-pop. He wounded or killed a few more. Some shots came out of the jungle, and he returned these, but nobody could get position to return fire. This all happened in seconds. It took me that long to cover the ground between us.

He was at right angles to me. I decided to go for a flying tackle; For some reason I thought he wouldn't shoot me. Instead, he reacted like a good soldier and sent me right over him by falling backwards and kicking me in the groin as I went over the top. Landing face first, I just lay there trying to deal with the pain. Through my mental haze, my ears told me he was still firing. Pop-pop-pop. Men screaming. Men falling. Men dying.

I opened my eyes and saw him about ten feet away from me. Off in the distance, I watched as a soldier stood up in the clear to try and get a shot at him. Drummond shot him dead. I reached for my holster and withdrew my 45. Slowly, I brought it around in front of me to a point where the butt rested on the ground and the barrel was pointed at Drummond.

I pulled the trigger twice, and the shooting stopped.

Of course I killed him at that range.

It was strange, even after the shooting stopped, no one moved for a while. Twelve solid seconds of automatic rifle fire can seem like a lifetime.

But I had felt that before. Post firefight. I was amazed to be alive after a fierce minute of death in the form of raining greased, lead projectiles.

Then I heard the moaning and the screaming and I became a soldier again. I got to my feet. They were all looking at me. They knew. There was no doubt I'd done it. I called orders to organize. Anh Dung came out of the shadows and I ordered them to call for medical dust-offs, two or three, I told him get going. He didn't say anything, just looked at me, then he went to the radio shack.

Looking down, I realized I was still brandishing my 45. It was still warm in my hand. I re-holstered it.

He had killed seven and wounded eleven. Lucky numbers, huh? I was ordered to fly out with his body. Anh Dung took command with Cao-Ly and promised to remain at the base until they heard from me. I never saw or heard from any of those men again, and I don't ever expect to.

They put me in isolation for two weeks while an intelligence team went into the field to investigate. They confirmed my story. I was cleared of any wrongdoing. But was ordered to remain silent on the matter. This journal will be my only record.

I asked for Stu's stuff, and they gave it to me. I've read all his letters from home. I know where and how his family lives. I know his son's name is Stuart, too. I know his wife's name is Sarah. I

*know everything about them, much more
than I wanted to know, really*

*As I said at the beginning, I've been
in Japan for a while now, in some Goddamn
silent Zen clinic. It took me a while
to get used to the continual quiet, but
I'm used to it now. For a while, I guess
they were nervous that I'd go crazy because of having to kill Stuart. I'm not
crazy about it: I mean I'm upset and
I feel responsible, but I'm not losing
it or anything. They told me they sent
Mrs. Drummond word that Captain Stuart
Drummond was dead. They said Drummond
had died bravely in the course of duty
behind enemy lines. They asked me to com-
ply with this story for obvious reasons,
and I said I would.*

*Couple more weeks and then it's home
for me. Word is we're pulling out of Nam
anyway. Kids at home yelling loud enough,
I guess. I haven't been stateside for six
years. I don't have any plans. Maybe go
back to dealing in turquoise and such,
like my dad used to. We'll see.*

*Drummond's family is from Colorado
too. So maybe I'll try to find them when
I get home. I'd like to talk to Mrs.
Drummond. I don't think I'll tell her who
I am, or the whole story, I think this is
the last time I'll do that. I'm just going
to see what I can make out of the ending.
I think I need to do that, at the least.*

I closed the journal and put it back on the table where I'd found it. Had Michael left it there for me to find? And at that second, within my heart, I made a silent pledge to myself to try and do something to resolve this situation. Then I finished packing.

During the night, a dream: two shirtless lumberjacks are felling trees deep in a sun-dappled forest, each wielding a sawdust-spewing chainsaw as long as a Viking's sword. Slicing deep into a trunk, one man finishes the back cut on a two hundred foot fir. But as he pulls his blade out, a robust gust of wind punches through the whole forest sending thousands of dead leaves whirling airborne. This sudden onrush of wind splinters the stump-shot, the only remaining wood plug holding this tree upright. As the stump-shot shatters into a shotgun blast of splinters, the massive Georgia fir snaps off its base, and hops away like a colossal pogo stick. The cutter dodges death by leaping off the ax man scaffolding remaining around the root trunk. But as the massive tree trunk skips away, the top swings far off its bedding path, out of its falling circle, and into the formerly safe region occupied by his partner. The first cutter's voice cannot carry over the popping combustion of his friend's flaming exhaust chainsaw, so his screamed warning goes completely unheard.

Chapter VIII

A former church retaining its steeple: now renovated into art and retail space and surrounded by newer buildings in the north end of Manitou Springs, Colorado. The busy Main Street sidewalk pushes past this old church's weathered grey planking, and around an adjacent ancient graveyard. On the second floor, black curtains are draped within a half-oval window. The words ROLL'N STONE are etched into the glass in an arch across the dark curtain background. Above this picture window, just below the roof's peak, is a small round, stained-glass window, half white, half black, swirling in a circle. In the back, a greenhouse-like dormer punches out of the steep roof and reflects the blindingly bright sunlight of dusk. On the street level, ornate double-doors open in invitingly. Below, a deep stone cellar breathes out cool air so powerfully that pedestrians often stop and enjoy a moment's refreshment. Some venture in.

Michael and I lease half of an old Catholic church on Main Street for our stone business; the other half of this planked chapel is rented by a local stained-glass craftsman. I practically never see him.

My stone-cutting bench looks outward from the glass dormer on the second floor. Through its glass I watch the whole length of Manitou while I work. I can also see the thick swaying low growth of evergreen and aspen trees on the first slope of the Rocky Mountains. It's a sunny southern exposure, so I have many plants up there, almost as many as grace Sarah's sills, but not quite. In the winter the studio is usually warmed by the sun so that I never have to fire up the pot-bellied stove in the corner; passive solar heating keeps the place cozy.

Michael and I rebuilt this place ourselves, store and workspace. Display cases are on the first floor, along with a small office for Michael. An exterior side stair leads up to my shop. It's all bare unpainted wood; we also bought an old, rustic grey barn for three hundred bucks, disassembled it, and turned it into interior walls.

The thing I like best about the store is a macramé archway about eight feet long that frames the entrance. It is very detailed and has feathers and planters and ribbon and ceramics in it, all very intricate. Sarah made it in a week. She also made the curtains that cover the office door: twirling palms in front of a sun swallowed in concentric heat circles. A line of her dripped wax makes a leaf, leading away in perspective; you really have to look at batik a while to appreciate it. Details reveal themselves slowly.

My studio has a kitchenette and a bunk, so I'd been living up there for a week. In the mornings, I cut up new Tiger's Eye into cabs. I would slice a three-pound rock like a loaf of bread; then, on the irregularly shaped flat plate, I'd lay out as many ring-sized stones as I could fit with the least waste. Then cut them out.

Shake had gotten me the gig. It was high quality Tiger's Eye, and I was getting paid very well, so I could afford to take my time. Those are the best jobs—good money at your own pace.

Once in a while, someone would come in below to browse the display cases. Everything was locked up, so I wasn't worried about thieves. Besides, the open door and hidden proprietor keep a lot of dishonest people honest. There's a press bell if they want service.

About noon, I looked up at the town clock as it sounded. Almost simultaneously, the bell from the store sounded repeatedly. When I got downstairs, I found Stuart kneeling in front of one of the cases.

"Hi, Paul," he said, looking up through the counter. "How are you?"

"Fine, Stuart, you?"

"Oh, fine. Mom will be here in a minute. She's at the health food store." He was eating a banana and offered me a bite. I took one and tried to return it.

"Keep it, I have another one." He pulled out a banana that had been dangling from his back pocket. "These are nice, Paul," he said pointing at some amber necklaces. "What are they?"

"That's amber, Stuart. It's tree sap that's hardened over a million years."

"Wow, can I see it?" I took out a necklace and handed it to him. "It's so light," his voice soft with wonder, "like nothing!"

"They're still stones, though."

"These are rocks?" Amazed, he carefully handed the necklace back to me. "Did you make it?"

"No, I bought it from a friend who is a sailor. He got the amber in Haiti and made it himself."

"Wow," he said again, his attention still on the necklace as I returned it to the case. "That would be nice for my mom. I think she would like amber: tree sap that has hardened over millions of years."

His taste surprised me. The necklace was one of a kind. Round, orange pieces captured around the edges by silver wire and strung with twirling hinges. The necklace would look spectacular around Sarah's neck.

I thought to myself to give it to him, to give to her, but just at that second, Sarah walked in the double doors.

The sunlight was so bright outside that a hazy brightness surrounded Sarah when she entered and paused just inside our doorway to allow her eyes to adjust. Sarah's simple white dress was cinched to emphasize her waist, making her a vision framed in our macramé arch. I had only seen her once, briefly, during the last week.

"Hello," she said, smiling. "How are you doing?"

Her emerald eyes were dancing happy and welcoming, and she looked directly at me. She could not control her grin and for the first time I felt almost certain she had feelings for me. My heart tripped and then increased in speed.

"Fine, been working mostly," I said, un-calmly.

Stuart turned back to the display case, shielding his amber necklace. Even though most of the jewelry was brand new, things she hadn't seen before, the display cases didn't seem to interest her in any way. Her eyes stayed up and looking around the store. It took me a second to realize she was looking for Michael.

"Michael's not here," I said, finally.

"Good," she said. Warm eyes settled on mine evenly and I felt a shock wave pass through me; it almost betrayed itself into a physical shudder, but I squeezed the case and sent it down into the floor. Her face was glowing with the blush of outdoors. For the first time, I noticed strands of silver within the wave of her pale hair, and a few shallow lines threatening her eyes.

"How's business, Paul?" She asked.

"Not much today, but yesterday, I did really well. Sold a lot of small pieces. Listen, come on upstairs, I don't have to stay down here." I led them up to my shop.

My workroom is the church's attic. The ceilings slant at the same steep angle as the outside roof so there's only headroom along the center spine of the space. Stuart wasn't affected and immediately began exploring the edges of the studio where boxes of stones and tools were stored. Sarah sat in an easy chair in the light from the glass dormer. The frames threw a shadow over her features.

"Were you working, Paul? I hope we didn't interrupt." She began to swing the chair gently back and forth in a rhythm, her yellow hair spilling out behind her. Her angel-white dress popped a front button and her body was there to see like a beach afternoon, sultry, sunny and hot.

"No, I'm glad to see you." I turned and began to wrap up my work. "I work in the morning, mostly, early." In a moment, I was through and washed my hands.

"Sarah, put something on the stereo."

"I don't mind the quiet if you don't."

She was right. Silence climbed up and down empty music scales in my mind, soothing and pleasing.

Stuart was giving the place a thorough going-over: opening drawers, unpacking crates. I noticed he became very interested in my wood carving set. One by one, he examined the beveled edges of each tool and then returned them to their canvas apron.

"Stuart, take a look at this one." He stopped and followed me to a low-hanging spice rack on the near wall. The third drawer was the right one, and I found my oldest pocketknife. It was an old-timer, beat up, but still holding a keen edge. I felt a little silly giving it to him, but I did anyway.

I placed it in his hand, and his palm didn't close for a full minute.

"Is it mine?" he asked, finally.

"Yes," I said, and I found him a hunk of soft pine. He dropped to his knees on the spot to try it. In a moment the floor around him was littered with curling white shavings.

"Thank you, Paul," he said, after a while.

I had iced tea, but Stuart didn't want any. Sarah and I sat together without speaking for a few minutes. She took out a cigarette and lit it. The quiet was a comfortable cushion for whatever thoughts we were both having. At least that was what I thought.

"Sometimes I don't know what to say to you, Paul. It's not unpleasant. It's just that I don't want to talk about the weather with you. You know what I mean? Does that make any sense?"

"It does. And I hear you, and I see you, and I feel exactly the same way."

I paused and that musical silence again filled my head. Comfort in silence is a feature of love.

"But I can't help thinking about Michael," I continued. "I can't imagine this is doing him any good."

"Have you seen him lately?" she asked. Her usually soft green eyes now had a sharp edge.

"No, I haven't," I said, "I've been staying here."

"Well, neither have I. And I don't mind that at all. The last time I saw him, he told me to do as I pleased, because he was going to. Can you imagine saying that to someone you love? Well, he said that to me."

"He cuts quickly and deeply," I added. "Never fight with a former soldier."

Sarah sat up quickly as if about to say more, but then, thinking better of it with Stuart in the room, she relaxed, and leaned back again.

"He probably went out of state for a while," I ventured. "He wasn't in very good shape when I last saw him."

There was another pause where musical silence filled my head. Then "he still has lots of stuff over at our house," Stuart interjected without looking up from a box of pitons. Then he crawled over to the other end of the room where there were more boxes of rocks to explore.

"Yes," Sarah added, finally. "He does."

"Well, he'll be back soon if I know him, and broke. He may have seen more action than I did, but I know him now, clear through."

That comment didn't lighten things up one bit for Sarah. I was simply staring at her now. She had finally noticed the new jewelry in the cases and was inspecting it when she suddenly looked back up at me, fully, into my eyes—an utterly beautiful and natural woman, focused completely on me, and gazing directly into my eyes. It was incredibly exciting, and I scolded myself for not being able to handle it better.

"Will you come to dinner tonight?" Her voice was low, almost a whisper.

"Yes," I said instantly.

"There are things I wanna say to you, Paul, so I'm just going to say them. You may think I'm terrible, but I'm not. Not when you know me. And I want you to know me, Paul. And I want to know you. It's not that I feel any less for Michael. And please don't think you've taken me away from him. I'm not his anymore, and he knows it. Now I want you to know it, too. Please Paul, please understand. I'm my own person. Can you detach Sarah from Michael? Please look at me." I turned around to face her directly and I looked. Her sun colored hair shimmered in the half-light, her dress's top buttons were open so I could see her breasts heave with emphasis, and the seductive scent of frankincense in her hair wafted over me like a caress. Then, suddenly, she clasped my face within her strong craftswoman's hands.

"I am looking at you."

"Well, then see me."

Here she is, sitting in my workroom, I thought, this chiseled woman of nature, this earth mother, hippie-goddess and the clicking tick of jealousy entered my stomach for the first time.

"I see you," I said, my entire nervous system at attention.

"I'm not sure you do," she said.

"Perhaps I'm no better than Michael."

"Oh, but you are, Paul. Not better, maybe, but at least further along."

"What does that mean?" My heart was pounding so hard I thought she would hear it.

"I think you know." Her cool voice never wavered.

"Paul, what are these?" called Stuart. He was dragging a box out into the light. I went over to look.

It was filled with miner's gear I had bought in Leadville. He put on a miner's cap and I turned on the lantern on its brim. The beam shot around the room wildly as he wiggled his head.

"What is this stuff for, Paul?" He asked.

"I use them when I go spelunking, which is going down into caves. I also carry a flashlight, and bring candles in my belt."

I put the web belt on him. The handle of my ice hammer almost touched the floor. He took one step and it was around his ankles, tripping him.

"You went down in a cave?" He looked up at me.

"Yeah, we used to go a lot. Strider went down with us once. He didn't like it much though."

"I want to go, Paul. I'm not scared." He returned to the box. "And there's plenty of helmets in here. Michael and Mom could go, too."

"No, thank you," said Sarah. "I'll stay right here on the surface. And I don't think you ought to go either, Stuart. Have you thought about what it's going to be like down there?"

"Dark!" he said with eyes wide. We both laughed with him.

"Is it safe, Paul? I mean he's only ten." Her eyes beckoned me for guidance and her voice had a slight tremor.

"Sure. Besides, I'll rope him up. There are only a few places where there's any danger. It would be a great experience for him."

"In a cave!" she exclaimed, and I immediately thought she would not let him. But Michael had told me that Stuart's dad had been a real outdoorsman and that Sarah wanted the same for Stuart.

"I would feel better if you both went," Again her voice betrayed a tremor. "Michael too, I mean. You could ask him to go with you when you see him next."

"Sure," I said. "When I see him next."

It was about twenty minutes later when I heard Michael come in downstairs. I knew who it was by the crack of his knees and the pace of his footsteps. Then he was at the top of the outside stairs where he paused in the studio doorway, his long arms locked bracing himself high up on the frame. Motionless, we all looked at one another from three separate points of the room, Stuart held within the triangle.

"I was in Albuquerque," he said.

"Oh," I said, and had to smile. I knew him so well now. He always left the state to cool himself down.

"How's business?" he asked. Sarah turned away at his question to look at my workbench, inspecting my just-cut Tiger's Eye cabochons. I could see that her body had stiffened considerably since Michael had arrived.

"Great!" I said. "I've been cutting cabs for a dealer friend of Shake's. Real nice Tiger's Eye...did you get your money? Shake paid off last week like he promised. I left the cash for you at the cabin."

"Yes, I got it this morning when I got back. Thanks."

Surprisingly Stuart hadn't been distracted by Michael's arrival, and ignored him by continuing to explore the random boxed materials of our business, continuing to crawl around the periphery of my studio beneath the low, steep sloping walls and ceiling.

"Hi Stuart, how ya doing?" Michael asked, a lilt in his voice adding a positive effect.

"I'm okay," said Stuart flatly.

Most kids can't really hide their feelings very well, and just then Stuart had none for Michael.

"Hey Sarah, what about you?" Again Michael's voice tried to lift the question up with that empty lilt.

"I'm good, Michael," Sarah answered, brushing a lone strand of hair out of her eyes. "You know, you left a lot of your things at our house. I'd like you to pick them up."

"Sure, this week, no problem." His reply popped out quickly.

Then a new silence settled on the three of us. This time there was no music in my head, though Stuart's box searching did add a random percussion to the background noise.

For a moment I thought Michael was going to turn, descend, and leave, but instead, he came in.

"How was Albuquerque?" I asked him as he moved towards my bench to examine the cabochons I'd cut that morning. As he walked over, Sarah slid away before his arrival. Slightly disturbed by her departure, he ignored it by sitting down heavily in my chair to examine the work.

"Nice stones, Paul. Sweet shapes too. Yeah, Albuquerque was great. I stayed with John and Becky. They have their own store now and guess what? John shot a robber! He didn't have any trouble, either. The other jewelers made sure he wasn't even arrested."

"Jesus, shot him dead?" I asked.

"No, but the guy bled all over the store. The thief shot first, but he only got John in the muscle of his left arm—clean through-and-through wound. Very lucky. He was out of the emergency room in six hours."

"The Wild West," said Sarah.

"Yeah," said Michael turning around in my chair to face her. "So how have you been?" His voice softened noticeably.

"I'm fine," she said in a clipped manner. "Really good, actually. I made a big sale to a store in New York City and paid my rent for the next three months."

"That's great," said Michael.

"Yeah, great. It only took me three years to convince them." She laughed. Then her tone changed completely. "Listen, Michael, since you're back in town," she explained slowly, "Paul wants to take Stuart down into a cave to explore it. Apparently it's safe, and I suppose it is, but I'd feel much better if you both went. Would you mind?"

She knew he wouldn't. Her questioning tone didn't seem like her. She was inserting distance between them into it.

"I think it's a great idea. I haven't been caving for years. It'll scare the shit out of Stuart, but he'll love it."

"Oh my God, that doesn't sound good!" Her left hand fluttered to her throat and she look directly at me.

"No, no, I was kidding," Michael reassured her as he rose from my bench and headed toward the kitchenette. He looked healthier than when he left, his eyes were clear, his face looked rested, and his movement was smooth and confident again. Travel always cured Michael, never of the entire disease, but always of the symptoms.

Sarah was quiet for a moment, and then she followed Michael to the refrigerator where he was getting a beer. They moved near each other, but were careful not to touch. I was reminded of two well-piloted helicopters rigging a power line. After a moment, they began talking together softly. Not wanting to intrude, I turned my attention back to Stuart. He was trying on the mining gear again.

Outside, it was dusk and the studio was taking on light in dusty shafts. Stuart helped me repack the gear, and we sat on the floor watching the sunset.

"This is much better than our house," he said. I shared my iced tea with him and he held the glass with both hands like a chalice.

"You think we could go in a cave tomorrow?" he asked, looking up at me. "I'd really like to go tomorrow. Can we?"

"I don't know, Stuart. We'll see what Sarah says."

"How about Thursday?" Michael called from the kitchenette. "We could go Thursday, Paul."

"If it's okay with Sarah." I responded.

"Fine with me," said Sarah.

Stuart was very pleased to have a confirmed date. But as Sarah and Michael came over to sit beside us, I noticed the pleasure on his face change to surprise.

"All of you?" he asked, incredulous.

"No," said Sarah, her green eyes flashing. "Not me."

During the night, a dream: Sarah is climbing the snowy spine ridge of a peak far above the timberline. She is roped up to an indistinct figure trailing behind her. At one point, she loses her balance and begins slipping down one side of the col's steep face. Instantly, the form behind her drops quickly down the opposite side to a point where their weights offset each other. The line sustained between them goes taut, and her fall is prevented.

CHAPTER IX

A sandstone spur, made of dry red rock poking up out of the thickly timbered forest slope like the knob bone on top of a human shoulder. In the surrounding woods, a thin channel between rising stone walls opens toward the ancient oval cave opening. Three human figures: a man, a boy, and a man, all roped together in single file, enter this thin stone gorge looking from a distance like the Morse Code instruction: .-.-. Within a moment, the knoll swallows this message into its hollow cavity.

Michael led in, then Stuart, and I followed. Ten feet from the cave entrance he flipped on his carbide helmet light. Stuart and I did too. The path in was a ramp down. The only light came from the erratically moving shafts of our helmet lights. Stuart was silent. Awed, I think.

The first thing I noticed was the air. It was much colder than on the surface, and noticeably more still; completely windless and smelling like a dugout cellar. The air was now the same temperature as the chilled stone walls I felt as I made my way along. My helmet occasionally scraped against the rock ceiling.

The path turned into a natural stairway. Michael's headlamp caught my expression as I zoomed my hand-light up and down, examining the complicated forms and structure of the cave. We continued down. Occasionally, the rope between Stuart and me would go slack, and I would come up on him. He was so much like his mother, courageous, curious, trusting and vulnerable. I found him examining a damp stalagmite with its matching stalactite dripping down on it from above. His eyes were wide open, running his hands up and down and all over it. Smart hands that I could tell loved to learn. His exuberant smile told me he was thirsty for new experiences.

"You haven't seen anything yet!" I told him, and we kept going.

The stone stairway went down, turned, then suddenly opened up to a large, gymnasium-sized hallway; our hand-lights roved over hundreds of stalactites and stalagmites. This space was the interior of the entire red-rock knoll outside, a giant, windowless and dark cathedral, a space that both beckoned inward and warned away, simultaneously.

The roof was seventy feet up, and made of huge wedged-in boulders. We wandered around the cavern floor exploring, but still roped-up. Stuart seemed very comfortable scrambling around the boulders, but I did notice his breathing was getting heavier. I figured it was just because he was dressed so warmly.

"This way," called Michael, "we'll go further down to the King's Chamber, and then over by the river." His voice bounced off the cavern walls in staccato notes and tones.

I stewarded Stuart along, following Michael as we headed down another thin path. The ground was very dusty until the path finally opened onto a circular well-like hole with a thin ledge spinning down to the bottom. The hole was fifteen feet across, and rose and sank from us like an elevator shaft. The walls were damp; in some places even running slick. Stuart looked over the edge and straight away retreated to an interior wall.

"It sure drops a long ways," he said, looking up at me questioningly. I just smiled and after a beat, he smiled back at me.

To make our way down, Michael edged his way out onto the ledge and sidestepped down. I had the rope and belayed his weight by wedging my feet. When he got to a wide shelf, he would tug the rope and I would send Stuart along and we'd both belay him until he reached Michael. I watched the line feed out as Stuart edged his way down the thin ledge, but he never stopped, which is a good sign. Gutsy little guy, I thought.

It took twenty minutes for all of us to reach the bottom of the shaft. Down this far, the air smelled metallic, and for the first time, I perceived the swooshing sound of running water. We drank our own fresh water from canteens and Stuart got a chance to catch his breath.

"Are you alright, Stu?" I asked.

"Yes—it's just this air. Too thick."

He took out a metered dose inhaler and took two short puffs to clear his airway. I knew he had asthma and Sarah had warned me to watch for symptoms, but he seemed to be handling things all right on his own.

Michael was distracted flashing his light around our present spot. A silver gleam sometimes caught and reflected back a beer can.

"People sure leave a mess," said Stuart.

"Yeah, said Michael. "Actually, I think some of these are mine from when O'Choate and I were in here. I'll pick them up on the way back. If you two are ready, I say we head on down to the King's Chamber."

Stuart coughed for the first time. A raspy sore sound, but then he got up and we both followed Michael's lead.

Slowly, we strung out along a new path, still ramping down, but more gradually this time. I had grown accustomed to the blackness by now. This was probably the twentieth trip I'd made below a hundred feet, but each time, it took me a long while to get used to the darkness, going down into the blackness.

The tunnel we were following was headed down to the most beautiful room in the whole Rock Spur system. Unfortunately, because the room lies off a cliff face, the only access points are thin, worm-like tunnels.

Our path did just this—the ceiling came swiftly down to where we were all on our knees crouching, then lower and lower until all of us were slithering along like snakes.

About ninety feet into this tense worm tunnel enclosure, I began to feel an irresistible desire to stand up. Something the miners used to call "miner's worry." It always made me speed up and in a second, I was almost on top of Stuart.

"You okay, buddy?" I asked him.

"No sweat. He reached into a pocket and pulled out his inhaler. Putting it to his mouth he took another puff. In a second he was fine and we kept going. But after ten more slogs of crawling his pace slowed again.

"I don't like it here, Paul." His breathing was irregular, coming in huffs: "It's too small."

"Can you reach your inhaler?" I asked.

He didn't say anything but I could see him reach around to his pocket and take it out. Again I heard him pump out a shot and his breathing gradually slowed to normal.

"Can you keep going?"

"Yes." His voice was raspy but he started to move again almost immediately. I was trying to remember how much more of this wormhole remained.

In a moment, the light on his little helmet vanished around a bend and I felt better that he would make it out. But as I came around the same bend I could immediately see the soles of his sneakers, and I knew he had stopped again.

"Are you okay, Stu?"

"No. Can't breathe."

"Stu, I know you can do it. Just press on and we'll be out of here soon. I promise."

Again he started to move, his elbows dragging him forward in short bursts and then stopping again while he tried to fill his lungs with air.

"That's it. Nice and slow. You can do it." I encouraged him, inch by inch. It was agonizing, but at least he was moving. Then he stopped again. This time, when I touched his legs, they were frozen stiff and I could hear him taking in air in great violent heaves, with a squeaky moan escaping with each weak release of breath.

"Stuart? What's going on back there? What are you doing? Keep on going!" It was Michael, blaring away from thirty feet ahead in the tunnel. His voice was authoritative, shouting out these orders in clipped commands. I could see his hand-light illuminating the next corner of the wormhole searching for Stuart.

I spoke very softly. "Stuart, you are okay. I'm right here with you." He turned his head back to look at me. His breathing was unnaturally forced, frightened and coming in great hollow gulps.

"Can't---breathe---asthma---inhaler---doesn't---work anymore," he sputtered.

"Damn it, Stuart, answer me!" Michael yelled. He couldn't reverse his view to see what was going on.

"Michael!" I shouted out to him, "Stuart can't breathe. He's having an asthma attack! We've got to go back and get out of here!"

"It's a lot further back than it is ahead. Let's get him to the King's Chamber. It's huge and there's plenty of air in there, maybe he'll breathe better." Michael and I both knew this place like the back of our hands.

"Okay." I said and crawled up to be closer to Stuart.

"Get him going, Paul. The longer he just lays there, the worse it will get." Michael tugged the line leading to Stuart until it was taut at the boy's ribs.

"Easy, Michael!" I yelled. Stuart was still heaving, his face pale white, his hands clammy. His eyes stared back at me, but he couldn't speak.

"First of all relax, buddy. I'm with you now and I won't leave. Everything is going to be all right. We'll start moving again now. This tunnel is only a little longer and Michael's already at the end. Go ahead. It's not far."

He understood me, turned slowly and began crawling in the direction of Michael's flash- lit wall where the tunnel curved. Here the wormhole was barely larger than the inside of a steel drum. It took Stu a while to make the turn, but when he saw Michael's headlamp at the end of the tunnel that kept him going like a lighthouse beacon.

I followed closely behind him, gently giving his feet traction, until we reached the tunnel's end and emerged into another large cave room all together.

Here there was an even deeper shade of darkness, more difficult to penetrate. I could feel Stuart desperately wanting to stand up again, to stretch out his legs and arms so I released him and we all did, and it felt damn good. But then I made Stuart lie back down on my denim jacket on the dusty floor. Even here, his breath was still coming in broken sobs.

The King's Chamber is not as large as the stadium hall. Size is not its greatest feature; rather, it is the location of the room. The King's Chamber is placed like a rookery in a giant underground cliff face. From it, one looks down and out onto the largest, most majestic hall of all: the Water Hall, so-called because of the rushing water noises of the subterranean river that is its floor. The King's Chamber was the peak experience of the entire Red Spur Cave system.

And fortunately here, there was plenty of air. In a few moments, Stuart's breathing difficulties eased considerably. Michael stayed with him as I went out to the chamber's edge and squatted down to think. All around me, even in the pitch darkness, I could sense the enormity of this underground grotto. My shirt was damp with sweat, and the sudden breeze coming up from the river chilled me to the bone. We needed to get Stuart out of here quickly, I thought, it's way too cold. And this is Sarah's son!

"Michael, come here for a second." Michael left Stuart and squatted beside me.

"Point blank: we need to get him out of here and we need to do it now. He's scared to death; his breath will never normalize in that state."

"Well, he won't go back through those tunnels. I told him he has to, and he looked like he was going to bite me."

There was a pause. We kept our heads turned away so as not to blind each other with our helmet lights.

"Michael, he's just a little boy. And he's having an asthma attack. Asthma is triggered by nerves so please don't make it worse."

"I know, but he's going to have to go up eventually. Unless you want to drop him down into the river and float around until it decides to come out, wherever that may be."

"Yes," I said, "we can take him out into the creek."

"What?" Michael turned his light onto my face, then quickly away. It was as if what he saw there startled him. I felt my confidence rise.

"We can take him down into the river, rappel down, then dive under and take him out into the stream at the base of the knoll."

"Where would we come out? Did you ever do it?" He knew I was serious.

"Yes, in a way. We would come out in the deepest of the Seven Falls ponds. Dwayne and I found the opening from the pond side in once, but I think we can find it out from this side.

"This is a mad plan, Paul. Suppose you can't find it?"

"You two can stay up here 'til I do. If I can't, then I'll come back up and we'll use the tunnels."

"It's still crazy. How far do you have to swim underwater? I mean, he's got enough problems without having to hold his breath."

"I know, Michael, but it's a good forty-five minutes to the surface if we climb, and that's if he climbs.

It could take hours if he can't help. He could be outside in twenty minutes if we go through the river."

"Shit," he said. "Shit."

"All told, it's about twenty yards underwater, including the ten feet to the pond's surface on the other side."

"Fuck. I don't know." Michael sighed. Then, finally, "Damn it, I guess we have to try."

In a minute, I was roped up to rappel. Michael held me on belay as I took the first step backwards off the cliff. I bounced out and down. The surface was granular and cracked as my boots slammed in. The rushing river sound got closer and closer until I could see the texture of the water's surface in my headlight. Then I was in it. My jeans went tight around my legs, but it was only up to my thighs. I released my roping.

"Michael, I'm down." I could see his light wavering above me. "I'm going to dive now. When we came in, we were right below the chamber so it should be around here."

"Okay, Paul. We'll be up here."

I dove and found only the bottom. The water was cold, but I stayed under to orient myself. After a few dives, I figured out where the opening was. Sucking current revealed it. I broke the surface and yelled to Michael, "I think I've found it. I'm going to follow it to make sure it comes out. I may be gone awhile, so don't worry."

"Right" was the only reply.

Gulping a huge breath, I dove. My elbows bruised as I entered the water tunnel. It was pitch black, but I remember it was very straight so I swam ahead, full force, my climber's legs propelling me. It went on and on, until gradually I could make out the walls a bit, then the grey opening where the tunnel met the pond. Then I was out of it, up the ten feet to the surface faster than my lungs could expel my last breath.

The sky was a welcome sight as I exploded onto the surface of a small pond. For the couple lying naked on the shore, my sudden appearance was like a champagne cork popping.

"Hey!" yelled the man, bolting upright, which is probably the only thing he could think of to say.

"Don't be alarmed. I've just come from a cave behind this wall. A child with us is in trouble. An asthma attack. Please, please, go ahead to town and bring help! Oxygen!"

The man reacted immediately and stood up. He scoured the ground for his clothes and began to dress. The woman still sat on her blanket, amazed. I was getting tired of treading water.

"Please leave the blanket so we'll have something to cover him with. We'll go down the Bar Trail, so send help back that way. I'm going back inside now, okay?" The man was still trying to get his pants on.

"Folks! Answer me! Will you get help?"

"Yes," he called out, "yes, of course. Come on, Janet, let's go! We have to get..."

I gulped, dove, and headed back inside. The difference between air temperatures was astonishing. Outside, it was mid-seventies, clear and sunny. Inside, it was fifty degrees, stale and dark. A shiver ran through me as I hit the surface in the cave.

"I found it," I yelled. I swam towards the light 'til my feet hit the ground. Climbing out, I realized I was exhausted. It felt good to lean against the rock face.

"Okay, Michael! Send Stuart down!"

The river was slightly colder than the air. The current was not swift, but because of an irregular bottom, I had a little difficulty standing. Above me, I watched as a spot darker than the darkness dropped slowly towards me. Stuart was not holding the brake rope at all. Michael was lowering him.

"Keep your knees bent, Stu, push yourself off the wall. That's right, buddy," I coached. A little above me was a rock outcropping.

"Hold it, Michael, stop there. Stuart, grab on. Sit down on that rock and hold tight."

"Are we getting out? I want to get out of here." His breathing was still irregular and he was very frightened. His voice shook and he sounded about half his age. I could hear Michael above, already beginning to descend. He stopped by Stuart, untied him, and lowered him down to me.

"Arrrre wwwwweeeeee goinnnnng nowwww?" the shivering little boy asked again as I cradled him. He was scared and he was sniffling now.

"Yes, Stuart, we are going out. But first, we have to go underwater. You'll have to hold your breath and keep your arms tight around my neck. Can you do that for me, buddy?"

"Your neck?" interrupted Michael. "Are you crazy? You must be exhausted. I'll take him." Michael made movements to take Stuart from me.

"NO. NO. NO. No. No. Not with him." Stuart wouldn't let Michael near him. "I don't want to go with Michael. He called me a baby." His breath began to sputter again, this time in both anger and more oncoming asthma. "But I'm not a baby."

"No, of course you're not, Stu. But right now, my big buddy, you and I are going to dive down and out of here and come up on the outside again. Okay?"

"Okay," said Stuart. "But I'm not going with Michael. He called me a baby."

"Jesus Christ, Michael, what is wrong with you?" I whispered to Michael angrily as I slung Stuart around into a piggyback.

"Not the time," he replied. "Later. Now, tell me where this opening is and I'll follow you."

I described the suction of the current and that the tunnel was very straight. Michael wished me luck and watched as I waded in. Once afloat, Stuart was dead weight on my back.

"Kick with me, Stu," I said, and he did.

As we approached the far wall, I gauged my breath, preparing. Turning around to him I said, "Are you ready, Stu? Here's what we're gonna do. We both have to take the biggest breath we ever took in our whole lives and then hold on to it! Okay, buddy?"

He nodded. Tears had left streak marks down his cheeks. I wiped them away and hugged him to me as hard I could. He clasped me back hard, sobbing.

"It's okay, buddy. Now we need to dive down and swim as fast as we can to a tunnel that comes out on the other side of this rock wall!"

He almost smiled amidst his shivering. What a brave young lad, I thought.

"Now it's a long way, but together we can make it!" I hugged him again and I could feel his breathing ease. "Especially if you help by kicking with me. Can you help by kicking with me, buddy?"

I released him from the hug and he looked me directly in the eyes. "I can do it, Paul."

"That's the spirit, buddy!"

I slung him around over my shoulders again so he could lie on my back. He laced his fingers together in a clasp and then looped his arms around my neck. We were ready.

"Now take the biggest breath you ever took Stu, and pinch me when you've got it. Start now!"

I felt the pinch and dove down with all the strength I had left. Both of us were kicking furiously. When we reached the tunnel opening we flailed into its dark sucking entrance like spastic fish. Inside this watery wormhole Stuart's fear returned and he clasped my neck tighter and tighter. It seemed much longer than my first trip and midway through, I heard bubbles go by my ear.

Damn! Stuart had lost up his breath and was now sucking water. I spun around to face him, but he was holding on so tight it was hard. Finally I was able to pull his face close to enough mine. Quickly I squeezed his nose shut with my fingers and, covering his mouth with mine, I gave him the last of my breath. His chest filled up. I turned back around and swam hard, dizziness invading my consciousness. For a second I though I might die from lack of oxygen, but then I suddenly got another burst of power from some secret internal source.

Emerging from the tunnel into the daylight-topped pond I threw the yoke of Stu's arms off and scrambled headlong for the surface. I was swallowing water fast and knew if I didn't get fresh oxygen soon I would drown right here. The top was white and clear like a glass ceiling. When I hit it, I alternated between coughing and throwing up water. Stu popped up beside me with breath to spare. I have never seen a child smile so wide. Holding him close again, I swam to the pond's shore and pushed him out ahead of me. We both emerged covered in brown muck.

The woman was waiting with the blanket. She wrapped Stu in it while I collapsed on the bank. My eyes closed, sucking air. It took me a full five minutes to catch my breath and calm my shuddering body. When I opened them again, Michael was standing there dripping wet and looking down at me.

"Stuart's okay," he said immediately. "How about you? You okay?"

"Yeah, fine," I answered. "Now let's get him home."

CHAPTER **X**

A trail: a part in the trees leading west out of Manitou. Beaten brown, and wide from use, the Bar Trail leads out of town to the base of Pikes Peak and beyond. Laced into the first range, it crosses a series of streams by wire suspension bridges. This highest trail bridge is a water pipe spanning a deep, narrow valley. Two men are crossing this bridge. One carries a child, wrapped in a blanket, across his back and shoulders. Because the pipe surface is curved, his progress is slow, never releasing a grip on the cable railing. On the far side, a clot of people with medical equipment awaits the men. A young woman is already one-third of the way out on the bridge, seeking to assist them. The first man scolds her back.

As soon as I laid him down, they put the oxygen on him. There was nothing for me to do, so I went off to the side and sat down. It sounds crazy, but I wanted a cigarette, and I don't even smoke.

Sarah was kneeling next to Stu. He wasn't unconscious, just weak and a little dreamy. After a few minutes of oxygen, his color returned.

"Oh my God," said Sarah, overwrought. "This is my fault. I'll never smoke a cigarette again. As God is my judge."

I had carried Stuart down three miles from the Rock Spur pond; Stuart wouldn't let Michael near him. Michael was sitting just below me looking off into space. All three of us were as dirty as miners.

"Bastard! I hope you're proud of yourself, calling a boy who can't breathe a baby!" Sarah spat at Michael, remembering how he'd taunted Stuart in one of his drunken rages. Wrinkles of pain and worry twisted around her already puffy eyes "Shame on you, Michael! He's only ten years old! Shame, shame, shame!"

One of the paramedics turned from Stuart and gave Michael a dirty look.

"I'm so sorry, Sarah," I said.

"I don't blame you at all, Paul. Not one bit. Stuart said you were very kind to him!" She started to cry and her voice shook with maternal emotion.

"It wasn't your fault that he had an asthma attack. I blame myself! I never should have let him go! And I never should have starting smoking."

I wanted to take her in my arms and soothe her, but I was not sure how it would be taken by either Sarah, or Michael.

"I was a fool not to think that going down into a cave might cause an asthma attack. A FOOL! And that is my private failure as a mother."

This statement took the heart right out of her, but she pushed on. "But that's not what's upsetting me right now!" Her voice and features tightened into loathing. "It's him, him, him, him!" She pointed at Michael and sobbed hard with each word.

"I'm sorry Sarah, it just slipped out," said Michael. "My father used to call me a baby."

"Too many vicious things have slipped out of your mouth," she said, speaking deliberately for emphasis. "I don't care for you anymore, Michael. I don't want to see you again."

I didn't believe her, but then she turned to me with her green eyes blazing and lower lip quivering. "Please help me, Paul. Stuart doesn't need to go to the hospital, but I have to get him home quickly and I can't afford the ambulance. Couldn't we use your jeep? I saw it at the base of the trail."

"Of course," I said. I looked over my shoulder at Michael as we all headed down. He had paused, alone, looking out over this small pond that had saved Stu's life, his eyes narrow as slits.

We still had about two miles to the road. The paramedics pulled Stu along on a mountain stretcher, and I lugged the oxygen tanks and the other gear. I dawdled, waiting for Michael to come.

"Go," he said, "you want her."

"I'm sorry this happened, Michael."

"Bye, Paul," he said, curtly, not looking at me.

"Michael, none of this can be a surprise for you. You made this happen yourself."

"Goodbye, Paul," he said, again. Detached.

"Goodbye, Michael," I said, and I meant it.

CHAPTER XI

A small room: dark, save the orange pig iron embers of spent logs. Outside, the mass of the mountains looms crowned with the pin light of stars. Inside, a couple lay in each other's arms on a small sofa. The slow pace of their breath combines and fills the room as its only sound. Smiling, with their eyes closed, they are awake.

T o be so close to her after so long; it could only make me realize that I had been waiting.

It was strange and familiar at the same time. This has happened to everyone—to find yourself in a position, or situation, where your senses inform you that you've been there before. That's how I felt lying there. It pleased me and scared me both, more than a little.

141

Then something completely amazing happened. At the height of our love, at the point of mutual climax, she wept, openly and happily and deeply. She wept in sweeping beautiful sobs, but different from when she cried in dread and worry for Stuart at the cave. Here and now, these were tears of joy.

This was because Sarah sensed that I loved her and she loved me. And that was enough for us in that moment in time, just being so loved so much, each by the other. And I did love her hard that night, not physically hard, but I really tried to demonstrate my feelings to her in the most intimate and deep way, from the inside out.

There was a translucent passion between us; looking into each other's eyes was an exquisite thrill. A look that was a vibrating, living thing, composed of both our souls. And this piercing union had birthed her sudden, ecstatic tearfulness—a searing, shaking, sealing of both our souls had caused it, a feeling so intense that it would not be denied its damp release.

We lay together, speaking.

"Underneath his condition, I can tell he's very excited about his adventure," said Sarah. "He told me you gave him the kiss of life in the water tunnel. He told me you saved his life." Her body felt warm and even against me, a good fit.

"Yes, I did" I said, snuggling closer to her. "He's a great kid. I'm sure glad nothing came of it; nothing serious, I mean."

"Except now, he's crazy for caves! He never stopped describing it. He said the only part that scared him a little was when it was real tight and small, and he had to crawl like a worm."

Her son was now soundly asleep upstairs. We had brought him down the canyon to Sarah's, fed him, and put him to bed. Sarah refused to leave his side until his breathing had slowed down and eased into a deep sleeping peace.

Then she began to relax. That was hours ago, and now, relaxed no longer seemed appropriate.

"Yeah, that's where the asthma hit him. It's really claustrophobic at that point. A feeling of being trapped. I can't stand it myself."

"My God, I was so terrified at first. You must understand—my son lying there soaked through, filthy, gasping for air. I just didn't know what happened. Heaven help me, I didn't know what to think."

She became tense for a moment, and I could feel her diaphragm tighten with a sob. I squeezed her closer and she let it out slowly, not giving in to crying. I stroked her long, pale hair.

"It's all right, Sarah, and he's all right too. He's a lot tougher than you think. Everything will be all right, my love."

"Yes," she said, and shifted in my arms. The light made her cheeks bones prominent, as the edges grew brighter in the firelight. When she turned her face up to me, I kissed her, and she kissed me back.

Our lips were friends by now, and quickly sought out the sweet spots we had discovered in the hours of lovemaking already gone by. I was still so hungry for her I thought my thirst for her kiss might frighten her. But all was reciprocal and we fed on each other's needs in an ascending, rubbing, sweating, caressing, driving, animal-like way, finally exploding in a rite and ritual of raw love.

Outside, the wind scoured the first range, briskly rubbing the aspen and conifer trees surrounding the house.

Darkness had fallen and there was not one light on in the whole house.

"It's gotten late all of a sudden," she whispered after a few moments. Then there was a long pause. Finally she whispered again, this time in my ear: "You know that I love you too, don't you?"

I was having momentary lapses into a second's sleep and dreaming. When she spoke, I woke to the sweet sound of her voice in my ear. It was both very close and very far away, simultaneously.

"Yes," I said. "And I love you too."

We kissed again and small sounds escaped from her as she nestled her head into the crook of my neck. I could feel the air of her breath brush by my throat.

"Let's make love, Sarah," I asked, my body aching for hers again.

"Yes, let's," she said, and she turned to kiss me.

A couple of mornings later, I moved most of my stuff out of our cabin. Michael's cabin, I mean. It was his before it was mine, but it was mine, too. It all went down to the store. He wasn't around then, and I didn't see him for a while after that.

Business kept me busy. The work I had done for Shake's friend, a guy called Snakebite, had turned out well. It sold for him right away. He brought me a couple of pounds more rock, and I was cutting night and day. After that, I was pleased, glad to have some independent source of income. The store was really mine.

Sarah would come down and visit me in the afternoon. She rose early and did her batik, saying it was the best light to read the dyes in. Watching her work some mornings always put me into a trance. Her strong arms easily bore the long and heavy wax-laden brush, her agile fingers manipulating the flow of wax from this brush onto the silk material. Her deftness here reminded me of the cool feel of her fingertips on my skin. Just after noon, she would come by the store and up to my studio. Invariably, without my asking, she would bring me lunch.

As I ate, she would examine my morning's work of cut cabochons. Some stones she liked, some she didn't. I offered her any one she wanted. "No, no thank you," she'd always say.

I figured when I found something I really liked I would set it up myself and give it to her. Then I remembered the amber necklace; warm to the touch, timeless and ancient, and created naturally from the sap of trees. And it would go with what she often wore, a long batik skirt with a man-cut shirt, knotted at the waist. The whiteness of her shirt emphasized the deepness and health of her tanned skin. The amber necklace would reflect this wondrous shimmering beauty.

Today Stuart was with her.

"Still hard at work even though it's clear past one. So diligent lately, it's a little frightening." She laughed, pale strands of her long hair falling in front of her sparkling eyes.

"Thanks, my darling." My lunch was a sandwich and a bottle of good beer. "Oh yeah, I could use a cold one!"

I quickly popped the Heineken bottle cap off using only my tooth. Sarah was shocked; Stuart was amazed.

"Cheers," I said, and took a long cool swig.

"You always have a new trick," she said, her voice smooth and full. I grinned like a kid.

"Hey, Stu, that's one you shouldn't try. Okay, buddy"

"I don't want to." He was so emphatic we all laughed.

It was an especially humid day, but for some reason I had not noticed while I was working. But now that I'd stopped to eat, the heat fell on me hard and suddenly. I started to sweat.

"You should quit, Paul. It's far too hot to do any more work today, dear one." A small smile drifted over her lips. "Let's go down to the Loop for a drink. It's always cool in there, the walls are stone!"

"I'm all for it," I declared.

"We can also get the details about the Moffat's annual mountain party," she said. "Someone down there should know all about it."

"Have you ever gone up there before?" I asked.

"A couple of times. Everyone has. His ranch is way up on the Platte. It stretches right down to the canyon's edge. They usually have a band that you can hear for miles. It's all Moffat's land and his father's before him all the way back to the original land grants."

Stuart sat listening intently.

"How long does it last?" I figured this party would be the scene of the famous cockfights.

"Three or four days, but it's usually only incredible for one night: puppeteers, mime groups, every kind of contest. You really have to see it."

"Sounds great. When?"

"I don't know. That's what I mean. If we go down to the Loop, we can find out. Moffat is there a lot, so someone will know all about the party."

"How many people show up?" I started to wrap up my uncut slices. Sarah, quite naturally, began placing the cabs in my velvet case. My stones looked very natural in her hands.

"Hundreds come! Someone flew in in a small helicopter once. It took him about ten tries to land the thing up there, because it was so windy, but he finally got it down. You'll love it, Paul." Her voice was secure and deep.

It was really Stuart who remembered the amber necklace, because at this point he was desperately trying to signal me. Standing by the staircase, he was pointing down and then grabbing an imaginary ring around his neck. He pointed at Sarah then pushed away, as if to get her going to leave. I finally figured him out.

"Sarah, why don't you go ahead, love? I have to clean up."

"What do you have to clean up?"

"The display cases downstairs; the glass."

"Oh, okay. I'll see you over there. I'm going to the post office anyway."

As she was leaving, expecting Stuart to come, he spoke up.

"I'll stay here with Paul, okay?"

"Sure, if you like." She smiled at me warmly, comfortable enough to leave her son with me, and then she left. When Stu was sure she was out of earshot, he ran straight to me and said, "Paul, can I have that necklace for my mom?"

"Sure, Stuart. Let's get it."

We went straight down the outside staircase. Inside the showroom he went directly to the case where the amber necklace was and knelt down to look at it. I unlocked the case quickly and pulled out the necklace and gave it to him. I didn't have to tell him to treat it delicately. It reminded me of the time we had found a pond turtle together. Just like then, Stu turned the necklace all around in his hands examining it, then, finally satisfied, he lifted it up to me, as if to say "here, you have a look."

I looked at the marvelous material one last time and gave it back to him.

"I'm going to catch Mom before she goes into the bar. I don't want to give it to her in the bar. They don't like me in there."

And with that, he ran out, the amber necklace strung out over his shoulder like the flame of a torch.

It didn't take me five minutes to get all the cases clean, so I caught up with them just outside the Loop Lounge. They were a little ways from the front door and just standing, so I guess they were waiting for me. Sarah had the necklace on. Twenty clear, orange sap stones, each as light as a feather, strung out on silver thread around her neck.

She had just received this beautiful present from her son, a gift from a child to his mother, and she was extremely pleased. Stu was very shy. Once he saw me arriving, he kissed her quickly, said goodbye, and then, as he tore past me he said, "Thanks, Paul, She loves it!"

Sarah stood smiling, wearing her brand new amber necklace, with her eyes fixed upon mine, and that's how it happened that she was wearing it when we walked in.

CHAPTER XII

A bar, long, polished, mahogany, dimly lit: around it, the conversations are turning from the mumble of afternoon to the chatter of evening. The bartender goes to the interior end of this wooden island, and throws a hidden switch. Then she adjusts the volume, and music seeps in and fills the space between the occupied bar stools. A clamor rolls in from the poolroom through its wide, arched entry. Then the smack of shattering wood is heard, and splinters a foot long fly into the barroom through this same portal. Conversations lull briefly, but are picked up again quickly. Those nearest the doorway turn away with studied concentration as a man emerges from out of the poolroom, slaps a hundred dollar bill on the bar, and letting slip a snicker, immediately returns.

S arah's hand tightened in mine as we walked in. We both had to stop just inside the doorway to allow our eyes to stop-down to the dimness. It was a little crowded, but we found two seats at the bar.

"I haven't been in here since we went up to the canyon," said Sarah, "but it's just the same." Her knee rubbed gently against mine.

As we sat down, several people greeted Sarah. They were very friendly, some seeming to look a little longer at her today. There were a few folks I knew and greeted as well.

"I'm always surprised at how crowded it gets here in the afternoon."

"Well, Manitou is that kind of town, I guess."

Even in this dim light her new amber necklace gave her neck an orange luster. It warmed her neck in a golden glow, touching the small recess that I had only recently come to know.

"Well, what'll it be, lady and gent?" Krystina was the oldest bartender in town. Young men and women came and went, but Krys was always pouring some-place. A native Coloradoan, she was well-loved and taken care of by all.

"Nice to see you, Sarah." Her freckled, weathered face was pulled out into a grin. "We haven't seen you for a while. Michael's inside." She nodded toward the poolroom.

"Oh. Well," Sarah paused briefly, then continued, "I think I'll be having a Beefeater's and tonic."

"Right away." Smiling, Krys then turned her knowing eyes to me. You don't last long behind a bar if you can't add up two and two. "How 'bout you, Pauly?"

Somehow it bothered me a little to be called Pauly by a sixty-two year old bartender with blue hair.

"Draft," I said.

As she poured, she inquired, "How are you doing, Pauly? I hear your company with Michael is no longer up and running. Izat so?"

"Well, I guess that's so if you say so, but you probably know more about it than I do." Sarah was twisting about in her seat.

Krystina noticed but went right on pouring. The lens of her eyeglasses directly reflected the white light bulb overhead. Her specs swept up into rhinestone points on the outside corners—a masquerade mask.

"That's a dirty shame. You always seemed to have such a calming effect on him. God knows he used to get into terrible trouble before you two hooked up."

Krystina had known Michael since he was a boy, before Viet Nam, before Sarah, before me. She knew his dad and mom and probably their dad and mom. She was Colorado.

"He'll be all right," I said.

"He ain't doing so good so far," she continued, "Broke two pool cues already today. Oh, he pays for them right away. I'm not worried about that. And the sporting goods salesmen don't seem to mind. It's just that I've never seen anything put a person on edge quicker than having pool cues shattering all around the place. I just can't have it!"

I got the feeling I was being volunteered to do something, so I didn't say anything.

"You'll probably get a chance to see for yourself if you stay long. Are you going to have something to eat?"

"No, let's eat at my house," said Sarah, "I have something almost ready."

"Sure, sounds good."

"No food then?"

"No."

Krystina went away to serve a new customer and then slowly wandered back.

"Another draft, Pauly?"

"Just about." I finished what was left of my beer, and she replaced it. The noise from the poolroom rose to a roar and dropped down. They were not individual voices, but howls, roars and whistles. It was a noise that did not want to be ignored.

"Yeah," said Krystina as she folded her arms, leaned back against the rear shelf and into a "seen it all" look. "They've been getting louder and louder every day for a week. That fellow, Moffat, is with them." She explained, "Pays the check every night in cash. I guess he's tuning up for his mountain party."

"When is this mountain party?" asked Sarah.

"I believe it gets started tomorrow, but the big night isn't until Saturday."

"Are you going, Krys?" Sarah asked.

"Of course, wouldn't miss it. Go every year. My beau Cooper takes me. We camp. One year it was so cold Moffat let us use one of the outbuildings, a line cabin. We were cozy in there, let me tell you!" She leered and laughed, but then stopped smiling abruptly.

"But what I'm seeing is—Moffat, and Michael, and these other boys have been getting drunk in here for days. What kind of shape they going to be in by Saturday?" She paused to emphasize her point. "I'm afraid I know."

Sarah was silent.

"Are you two going up together?" asked Krys, smiling again.

"Yes, I guess so," I said, a bit haltingly since Sarah and I had not discussed it.

Sarah looked over at me and smiled. "Stuart would probably love it," she said, and I nodded.

Krys smiled and spread her hands wide on the inside rail of the bar. "It'll be great fun to see you two up there, I mean three, there, including your son, missus." Krys winked and went away to help another customer.

Michael.

He sat down at the opposite end of the bar calling for twelve beers. Although the temperature was cool, Michael was sweating. It took him a moment to spot us. I swear I saw his face soften at first, as he looked at us, but by the time he made his way around to join us, his mood had changed.

He stopped behind us and just stood there looking directly at Sarah's back, silently and intensely. Turning to see him, it took me a moment to realize he was not looking at her, but at her neck and her new necklace.

"Paul, I want to talk to you alone for a minute," he finally said, slurring a little.

He was in that pre-drunk state of mind where mental faculties are beginning to shut down, but physical abilities are still operational. He backed up and walked toward the door and out.

As soon as I stepped outside, he was right there in my face, maybe three inches away, morphing into predator mode in an instant, and this time I was his prey.

"How is it, Paul, how is it that Ms. Drummond is wearing that amber necklace?" He spat this out at me with airborne droplets of spittle wetting my face. "Did someone *give* her that amber necklace? The amber necklace that I was saving, that I had almost sold? Huh?"

Michael's eyelids blinked rapidly like the strokes of a drum roll. I wiped the spittle off my face as I stepped back.

"Stuart gave it to her," I said very slowly. "He asked me for it, to give to her. So I did. I know you got it from Tom and there are no more left, but I didn't think you'd mind Stuart giving it to Sarah."

I breathed evenly and was totally calm, staring back hard into his agitated eyes and contorted face.

"Oh," he said, eyes narrowing, then dimming and easing. The anger that had possessed him to his core drained out of him like a camp cup with a hole in the bottom, his adrenalin surrendering to alcohol. "That kid's got expensive taste," he said finally as he backed up to lean against the stucco wall of the bar, now needing its support.

"Listen, Michael, since you're telling everyone else that our partnership is dissolved, you might as well tell me to my face," I added, my own anger rising.

His facial features hardened back up; his trigger pulled, he reverted to type. But, now, with the adrenaline gone from his bloodstream, the liquor hit him hard and all at once and he was really drunk and slurring his words.

"Fine," he finally garbled out. "Then listen up, 'cause I don't repeat myself. Our partnership is over.

Terminated. You take the store. You take Sarah. You take Stuart. You take it all."

"Doesn't have to be like this, Michael. Let's talk. Can you do that? We'll go back inside, take a booth, and just talk. I know more about this than you think I know."

"Forget it. I'm not talking to you, or her, or to anyone. Get away from me." He pushed past me heading back into the bar. Sarah came out at the same time and he almost bowled her over.

"What was that all about?" she asked as I sat down on the curb. Her voice quivered.

"The opposite of a merger."

"What is it with him? He's such a puzzle when he's like this." Carefully she reached around and rearranged her braided mandala bun.

"I don't know. Better just wait it out. His binge will end soon and I'll talk to him then."

Sarah had never brought up Viet Nam or her husband so I couldn't figure a way into it. But I wanted to confess. I wanted there to be absolutely no secrets between us. I wanted to tell her all about Michael's combat journal, about Michael and her dead husband. But I also knew only Michael had that right. Only Michael could tell her.

"It frightens me," she said, "how much people can change."

I saw a shudder pass through her body, a brief tremor, although it could have been just the freshening night air.

"The circumstances changed, too. That had a big affect."

She fell silent for a second then asked, "You are no longer in business together, then?"

"Temporarily."

"I feel a little guilty, but not much," she said and giggled, her laughter filling with mischievous mirth. Then she turned those powerful green eyes upon me like a beacon. "I mean, I haven't talked to him in weeks. I kind of miss him."

"I know. Me too. But I think it'll all work out."

"How do you know that, Paul?" There was no malice in her voice, just a simple, honest question. It was almost as if she somehow already knew Michael's secret and had accepted it. But then she was so different from any woman I had ever known. Knowing. Loving. Grounded. My eyes dropped onto the batik scarf she was wearing and the mandala pattern that repeated all over its soft silk.

"I guess I don't."

"Then let's go home and see Stuart," she said after a few moments. "We can tell him about the mountain party."

"Okay," I said, as we rose from the curb.

"Good evening, you two," called Krystina.

The dim evening light was darkening into the murk of night where my tired eyes painted everything a luminous white. Sarah took my arm, and we started to walk home. Her exquisite silhouette glowed luminous and bright, and chills ran through me as her fingers clasped firmly into my upper arm.

"Are you cold?" she asked.

"No, not anymore."

As we turned a corner, I pointed out the waxing moon to her, but her mind was elsewhere. Distant. So I stopped and turned her toward me. I held her slender neck between my thumb and forefinger, and tilting her face back up toward me, I kissed her hard. Lips upon welcoming lips, bliss wrapped up in a silken scarf, my heart suddenly beating beyond my own body. I realized in a flash that I was now in this completely. Some of my thoughts returned, but not all.

CHAPTER XIII

A cliff-edged road, dirt and thin, and cut into the mountain's steep side like a railroad switchback. On it, two vehicles noisily climb up the last of a series of ascending ridges to a narrow pass. Above them, along the final approach, a string of parked cars, Jeeps and pickup trucks defend this last, final incline. Over the top, on the far side of this gap, runs a long, broad strip of grassy meadow, walled in by black-green conifers and running softly down for miles, coming to an abrupt end with a craggy precipice high above the Platte River. A plane circling noisily above this hidden glade cuts its engines for a moment and two specks drop out and down. The crowd below hushes as all attention focuses on the descending parachutes.

161

It was a long way down outside the passenger window. The road was ledged and hugging close in to the mountain. We bounced high in the cab as the truck went up and then over the lumpy rocks. Moffat's property was about twenty miles out of Manitou, almost all on one-way mountain roads.

Now on the final pass, Sarah laughed and pointed up through the windshield into the cloudless sky.

"Look," she exclaimed. "Parachuting into the party! That's wild. This is going to be great! I want to fly too!"

I looked with amazement from her to the colored chutes as they tilted and roved about in the sky above us. As Shake's truck cleared the pass, they were lost behind the tops of the trees along the ridge's spinal crest. I turned to look through the cab's rear window and saw Stuart sitting next to the wheel well, staring off to the spot where the parachutes had disappeared. His eyes were wide as hubcaps, but he was still holding on tight to the pickup bed's wall. Strider leaned against him.

Shake was giving us a lift to the party. He had traded in his muffler-less Chevy for an old-school four-wheel drive pickup, and he was in his glory. Following us was a charming old Mexican gent towing a trailer. Moffat had asked Shake to make sure this fellow got out safely to the party. We were all pretty sure the trailer contained fighting cocks. The man's name was

Mr. Enrique Mero, and we had been formally introduced to him that morning in Manitou.

As we came down the far side of the pass, the view of this pasture was spectacular; spread out everywhere were many colored tents and tee-pees. A new, crudely built windmill was off to one side, surrounded by perhaps three hundred parked motorcycles. Spotted throughout the gathering were several large kitchen shacks breathing out cooking smoke. There were also two wooden stages, and one high-walled circus-style tent. Crowning the meadow was what appeared to be a plywood castle. Scattered among these structures were people, hundreds of them of all kinds, shapes and sizes.

"Wow!" said Sarah. "I just can't believe it. I've lived in Manitou all my life, and I've never ever even heard about this place."

"This place is a bit out of the way," Shake interjected. "We left the Gold Camp road about eight miles back."

As Sarah leaned forward to watch the reappearing parachutes land, her exquisitely braided mandala bun again caught my attention. Today she had woven a strand of mountain daisies into it—white and yellow flowers circling within it like a wreath. I couldn't help myself and sighed with pleasure at the sight.

She heard, looked over at me and smiled. Her eyes melted me like a callow candle.

"Where do we park, Shake?" I asked, trying to pull myself together.

"I know a special place. It's up along the western tree line. I've been coming up here for years."

Shake then looked in the rear view mirror and remembered Mr. Mero behind us. "Jeez, I forgot. I'm supposed to escort Enrique to the main tent right away so he can sign in." He quickly pulled over.

We all got out and walked back to Enrique's car. The Mexican drove a 1950 Chevy Deluxe and was now pulling heavy canvas covers off his cages in the enormous rear trunk. He had kept it roped open for the trip up so his birds could have fresh air. The creatures were obviously upset about the rough journey and were squawking loudly. Mr. Mero spoke to them in Spanish and they quickly quieted down. He wore an impeccably tailored double-knit suit, and was sweating, but didn't seem to mind.

"Well, Paco, what's the story?" asked Shake.

"My name is Enrique, Senor," he corrected. "And my birds aren't used to such a drive."

"Sorry, but there are only two ways in, and that was the easy one."

"It is of no concern; my birds are all well now. Where is the pit?"

"It's in that tent there near the main house." Shake pointed directly across the meadow to where a long, thin, ancient mountain building stood. Beside it was a large green military-issue tent. "Moffat said to tell you he'd have a room set aside for you in the house."

"That is excellent," said Mr. Mero. "I will go there now."

His old black Chevy cut an interesting profile against the natural lines of the woods, definitely from a different era. This morning I had noticed that he was living in the car. In the back seat area, he had a custom set of dresser drawers built in, and the foot-end in the trunk.

"That's quite a car you have, Mr. Mero. Did you build it yourself?" I asked.

"No, I had it built for me in Mexico when I first became a cockfighter. Many fighters in Mexico have cars like this."

He hopped back into the driver's seat.

"Perhaps I will see you at the fights," he said before he started up and drove off.

Sarah hadn't said anything, and I looked at her now.

"Amazing character," she said as we turned to walk back to the pickup. "Just amazing."

"Now are we going to camp?" asked Stuart, his frustration palpable.

"Yeah, now we camp!" said Shake. "You're gonna like this, Stu."

Shake sealed up the tailgate after Stuart and Strider had jumped in and we drove off to find Shake's special shady spot.

We set up camp near the top of the meadow on the lip of the surrounding forest, very near where we had first come over the pass. There was a panoramic view of the river canyon and all the ground leading down to it.

After setting up, we decided to walk down into the center of things and do some exploring. There appeared to be a clearing, midway down to the river's edge. We began walking along the woods but soon abandoned them to weave among the tents, trucks and teepees.

Some camps were thick with old trucks, circled up like Conestoga wagons, or pup tents spotted about randomly like an Indian village. Other folks choose to be off by themselves, like we did, along the meadow rim. People were of all ages, but mostly young. There were all types: long hairs, long dresses, miners in filthy jeans as slick as old calico, rich city people with shiny new Ford pickups, and mountain men in their plaid flannels. There were many earthy and naturally beautiful women that reminded me of Sarah. I was now tuned into these wonderful creatures. Nurturing, loving ladies that danced into a man's heart like a ballerina en pointe.

As we descended, we passed a fellow adorned in a Shakespearean shirt with huge bellowed sleeves. He had a Rip van Winkle beard and was wearing colorful eye makeup. Leaning back on the sissy bar of his motorcycle he called out to Stuart as he went by, staring back wide-eyed.

"Welcome to the gathering of the tribe, lad!" the biker said to him, smiling kindly.

"Thank you, sir," said Stuart, not taking his eyes off this sorcerer.

There were many children. So many that it sometimes seemed like recess on a school playground. Frisbees flew everywhere, their tossers moving amidst the crowd like dancers in a carefully choreographed ballet. One fellow kept his Frisbee spinning up into the air continually by skillfully tapping its moving center until we had passed him and he was out of sight, only his Frisbee bouncing up into the sky again and again.

Shake went off on his own and Stuart and Strider ran out ahead while I walked slowly behind with Lady Sarah, as I had come to think of her now. Sarah's hand gripped mine tightly as we roved along. She was greeted often, and several times introduced me when it seemed appropriate.

"Haven't seen many of these people for years," said Sarah, "Since Stuart joined the army, really." She paused. "The Green Berets weren't very popular then and a lot of people cut us off because of it."

Her jaw tightened, but I could also see her pride. She had loved her husband and his courage to do what he thought best at the time. Stuart Drummond had been her husband and she still loved and respected his memory and I loved her even more for that. I thought of Michael's journal and of how Lt. Captain Stuart Drummond had met his end. I quickly pushed that out of my mind.

Sarah straightened up and smiled up at me. "I guess I lost these folks for a while," she continued. "It's nice to be back. Thank you for bringing me up here, Paul."

Once again I had that terrible feeling of deception; of deceiving the only person in the entire world who I truly loved and adored; the only person who I should never have any secret from, ever. It felt truly horrible to know more about what had happened in Viet Nam then she did, about something she should know every single detail about. Maybe not, though, I thought to myself, since it would probably cause her more pain. There was simply no way I could "un-widow" Sarah. Her husband was gone and could never return. But I could love her. I could do that. Her radiant smile and trusting eyes upon me were all I needed as reassurance, at least for now.

We came up to the plywood castle. There was a big sign that said "Children's Castle, No Adults" but below it, in small letters, it said, "Well, maybe one or two." They had rigged the corners to look like turrets and the opening was made out to be a drawbridge.

An energetic clown wearing a sandwich board listing the events of the afternoon and evening danced about just outside: Mime and Marionettes, A Silly Drama, Magicians, and a Fireside Storyteller reading until midnight.

Directly in front of this rough wooden castle was a young long-haired saxophonist tapping out the delicious Joni Mitchell tune *Real Good For Free*, and that was exactly what he was doing, playing beautiful free music for all of us. His notes caught my ear and went straight inside me to the place where music rules the heart, filling the mountain air with perfectly rounded notes of love and freedom and beauty. I clutched Sarah's hand even more firmly, feeling in my heart, for the first time in my life, that I never wanted to let it go.

Sarah and I were both impressed by the musician, but for Stuart, the castle itself was the thing. He came running up to us, already excited and jabbering out his news.

"Wow, it's really neat inside! And they don't mind Strider barking, not one bit! Duncan is here too. And his mom checks on him all the time, and she said she doesn't mind watching me, too, and, and, and, they're going to have a puppet show in a few minutes! Oh, can I go, Mom, please? It'll be okay with Duncan's mom watching us! Please? Please? Please?"

It was the longest speech I had ever heard from Stuart. I let out a belly laugh remembering my own excitement when I was his age and found something of delight. His small honest face beamed up at us.

"Okay, my darling son," said Sarah, her smile widening with every word. "But you mind Mrs. O'Day and watch that Strider doesn't make a mess, and don't you dare go anywhere else. Do you know where our camp is?"

"Yup. Sure I do." He pointed up the meadow to where our camp was plainly visible. "And Mrs. O'Day will take me back up there if it gets dark. She likes to watch me, you know that."

"I'm not so sure of that."

"She does, Mom! Besides, Duncan says that they have a speaker that everyone can hear, so if your parents get lost, you can just call them and they have to come to the kids' castle and get you. Easy!" He squeaked in excitement and let out a joyous squeal. Then, not waiting for a reply, he ran off to join the knot of children lined up on the tent's drawbridge. Dust billowed up from this crowd of youthful energy as they introduced themselves to each other and slapped their high fives.

"Did you notice he said parents, Paul?" asked Sarah as we walked on. The smile on her face deepened and she wrapped her arm around my arm.

"I did. I did notice," I said in a whisper after a moment, hardly daring to believe the joy I was now feeling in the core of my self. Moving on, we made our way down among many more odd sites and sounds toward what seemed to be the center of this immense gathering.

Sitting outside our tent, I was pleased to hear the twangs of banjos tuning up. The stage was almost a mile off, but the speakers carried the sound up to us clear and true, if a little delayed behind the action.

Sarah was packing away the kitchen. Shake had eaten with us, and gone on his way, Stuart had left with Duncan for the castle, and I had just finished cleaning up the pots.

A fiddle run startled the bluegrass band into action, and a hoot and cheer went up from the gathered clan. Once again, I watched as many people scrambled down to the stage and clearing. It was dark, but the telephone poles at either end held giant lights with generator trucks nearby. In the arc of the blue light, I could see couples spinning, the women's dresses twirling. Sarah came out and sat beside me. Our hands quickly found each other.

"I love the view of the canyon from here," she said, not noticing the new goings on. "It looks like a scar sculpture cut deep into the land. But not a bad thing. Something beautiful and timeless."

"Paul, is that where we were today on the way up here?" She pointed to a place where the Platte canyon twisted through some "S" turns, and then straightened out again as it reached the high plains. She leaned into me as she pointed. We could just make all this out in the pale moonlight.

"No, that's a lot further away than it looks, Sarah. We only went there." I pointed to a spot about two miles down the meadow where we had thrown rocks into the Platte.

"That other place is Patna. We went there in the spring. Do you remember?"

"Oh, sure. With the inner tube." For the first time, she noticed the dancers. "Oh my, now they're dancing. Looks like fun."

"Would you like to dance, Sarah?" A thrill chill crept up my spine like a spider's path.

"Down there?" she asked, pointing to the field.

"That seems to be the dance floor."

"Paul, I haven't danced in ages." One of her hands fluttered nervously up to groom her beautiful hair. "What about Stuart though? Uh, well, yes, I mean, yes. Yes I would like to very much. Just let me get my shawl."

She was wearing maroon velvet pants and a white blouse. In an instant her fingers spun her long, long hair back up into a circular bun; that magnificent mandala that I now adored. Throwing on an antique black embroidered shawl, she pulled it close around her shoulders and was ready to go.

We meandered down to the noise of the dancing; two creatures of an exact moment immersed in sacred seconds, filled to the brim with music, laughter, and our own joyous heartbeats. It was ultra-moon-bright, and the stars backed up the dark tree line like a stage set. We met Mrs. O'Day on the way down and she promised to watch Stuart until we came back from 'dancin'. She smiled at me in the way women do when they know a man is in love.

"I just came from the castle," she said "and they're both still in there. The marionettes were really great. I don't know where Moffat finds these people. Well, you two just go along. I'll watch the boys."

When we were a little further away, Sarah told me Mrs. O'Day was a war widow as well. They had known each other a long time, and their husbands had known each other, too. It was strange to hear her say the words "war widow." Her voice changed briefly inside those words—a sad flatness filling them with a startling sorrow. But then it was gone and she smiled again. I was glad it didn't have the power to linger.

"Its really wonderful that Stuart has found someone to play with," she said.

Our old jeep was the first thing I noticed when we got down near the ranch house and clearing. It was parked next to Snake's truck, and right next to the cockfighting tent.

"There's our jeep, Sarah," I said, "So Michael's up here someplace."

"I figured he wouldn't miss this," she said, sniffing in a dismissive way as we walked past it.

By this time, we were so close to the speakers that we were practically yelling at each other. She grabbed my hand, and then giggling, she hauled me out into the crowd of dancers.

We danced country-style to about five songs, and that can really wear you down. Sarah is an elegant dancer. She's small and trim and spins like a ballerina. Her mandala bun was her personal signature, her spirit, her essence; real magic spun up into a perfect human design. Yes, that was Sarah. That was *my* Sarah.

I was glad when they finally played a slow song because I wanted to hold her. When it was through, we started off into the crowd of onlookers to find a place to sit down and relax.

That was when I saw Michael. It was like I knew he was there before I saw him. We passed each other, looking down so as not to stumble, then quickly looking up as we recognized each other's clothes, then pushing past each other before we could see eye-to-eye.

Sarah hadn't seen him, and when I turned around he was already eclipsed by the crowd. Together we made our way to a bonfire nearby and sat beside it. The aroma of marijuana floated on the night air like a powerful perfume.

"That was pure delight, Paul. You're full of surprises!" she said breathlessly after we'd settled. Flushed from the jig, her face in the firelight took on the glowing blush of the runner after the race, the explorer going over a new pass, the climber with her foot on the peak. It thrilled me into a tremor of pleasure, a body-quake of emotional recognition of how much I felt for her.

Close to Sarah in the dark night, I watched the bonfire reflected in her pupils. Our eyes seemed to stare directly into one another's souls. My heart was humbled by the power of her honest gaze; there was deep love in it, and pure unconditional acceptance. The courage in her eyes frightened me, somehow. Here, finally, was a person from whom I could never bear to be apart.

She tilted her head to the side, looking back at me quizzically, but I didn't know what to say. I put my hands gently on her cheeks and held her face up to mine.

"I love you, Sarah." It didn't sound as passionate, or romantic, or filled with yearning as it did hearing it in my own head, but it was exactly what I felt at that second.

She didn't say anything, but leaned into me and kissed me; heaven. It was a yielding kiss that ended with the two of us lying side-by-side, our faces close, our eyes wide. All sound and movement vanished.

"I need you, Paul," she said. She looked as if she was going to continue, to go on and say more, but she stopped, and then, choked up a little, began to cry very softly.

"Please hold me," she said, tucking her head in beside mine. We lay there silently. I felt her tears transfer from her cheek to mine and she held me with a strength that stunned me.

After a few moments, the noise and the crowd began to trickle back into my head. I guess the same thing happened for Sarah, because she pulled her head back, looked around, looked back at me and began to laugh.

"I feel like I just woke up from sleeping," she said. We both laughed and began rolling around in the firelight like children. She loved me! I was so happy.

"Again, Paul. Please dance with me again?"

"Yes," I said, and pulling her up, I led Lady Sarah out under the stars and back down to the dancing.

We danced to many songs, but I don't remember the name of even one; all I remembered were her green doe-eyes looking up at me from another world.

Then, as it got later, something shifted. The men began to move off towards the tent where the cock-fights were set to begin at midnight. People who had been drinking all day began to act up. Many women went back to their camps. For me, I could tell something was coming.

We were rocking back and forth, turning slowly together like swans to Joni's *My Old Man* when it happened: suddenly, it was as if there was a secret conspiracy within the crowd, because an alleyway cleared among the dancers right up into the surrounding crowd to a spot where a lone figure was standing, smoking, the glow of the cigarette ember in his mouth the only light. It was unmistakable. Lanky, strong, feet apart. It was Michael.

He was holding a whiskey bottle by the neck, swigging from it, and looking down at the dancers, at us. At Sarah and me. When he turned his face away to the bonfire, his eyes went pure red the way bears' eyes will when your flashlight catches them eating garbage. I could feel Sarah stiffen and shudder in my arms. I knew she had seen him too. And then the alley closed just as quickly as it had opened.

"Let's go," said Sarah, "let's go back to the tent. I need to check on Stuart."

I agreed and she took my hand, but we both knew why we were leaving the dance.

The expanse of cloudy night sky had lowered by the time we made it back up to our camp. Stuart was there with Duncan and Strider playing scrabble. Mrs. O'Day had just left, going off to get some pie before making her first attempt at bedding them down.

Stuart and Duncan spent the first ten minutes telling us all about their day's activities. When Mrs. O'Day returned, we all had apple pie and milk. Duncan asked if he could sleep over and Mrs. O'Day consented. So, having each other for company, the boys went inside their pup tent to go to bed. After fifteen minutes of whispered, conspiratorial conversation, the tent went quiet and all we heard was childlike snoring. Mrs. O'Day packed up the remnants of her milk and pie and said goodnight.

We were now alone.

The clouds above had crept in lower with the darkness, and were now sitting just above the treetops like a basement ceiling. We could still hear the dancing far below, and sat there quietly watching it. It was late, and I noticed that a lot of the fires that had previously dotted the hillside were now burning out and down. People were going to bed. Then, I noticed the crowd forming around the green tent beside the main house and I remembered the cockfights.

At just that instant, Sarah surprised me. "Why don't you go down there, Paul?" Leaning over, she slung her arms around my neck in a loose loop. "I'll be alright up here, and it's not likely you'll see another cockfight for a while." She paused. "I know you desperately want to."

I looked at her for a long moment and for the first time I genuinely recognized the age difference between us. The more I loved her, the more she amazed me with how deeply understanding she was about so many things, even including such masculine things as cockfighting. She was much wiser than I and I loved her even more for it.

Looking into her eyes, her heart felt so roomy then that for a second I wondered what it would be like to have a child with this woman? It was something I had never ever thought about before in my whole life.

This huge emotion was followed by such a rush of affection that I leaned in and kissed her hard. Parting my lips, I ventured in past hers to gently explore her mouth with my tongue. We kissed hard and kept on kissing, just four lips and pure loving imagination; so sweet and wet and exciting.

For a moment I thought about not going down the hill to the cockfights at all; I thought about staying right here with her and making love in our tent until sweat poured off us like running droplets after a river swim.

"I love to kiss you, Paul," she purred in my ear. Suddenly she stood up, pulled me to my feet and kissed me again. Then, just as abruptly, she broke off the kiss and again engaged me in a direct and powerful gaze. "Now I know Shake would never forgive me if I kept you from going to those fights. I don't understand the attraction of chickens killing each other. *In fact, I hate it*. But I don't guess I'm supposed to understand it. I just know that I love you enough to want you to be happy, even if it is in ways that I don't understand. So, well, get going! But please say something first, for Christ's sake!"

My newly kissed tongue and mouth tried to straighten themselves out to form proper words. But for a second I couldn't. That was Sarah's effect on me. Finally I could speak.

"Yes, okay, I'm going...but I love you, and I'll be back early. And if it doesn't rain tomorrow we'll take the boys and do something fun together."

She released her loop around me. I went to my pack to get some money—there was sure to be betting and, Sarah was right, I was really in the mood for it. Risk and violence and money really do go together, I thought. She laughed at me again, seeing what I was doing.

"Make sure you pick the right bird!" she said, grinning. I went back to her, kissed her again, very tenderly, and headed back down the hill to the fights.

A little way down, I stopped and looked back. I could barely see her beside the waning flames of our campfire, a fire that had been blazing only a few minutes earlier.

Chapter XIV

A huge canvas pavilion, walls tied up, Government Issue, and crushed with people entering from all sides. In the center of this cigarette smoky arena is a pit. Dug into the ground and protected by a low barrier, the pit is a wide circle of wood, eighteen feet in diameter. Two sets of "scores," three-foot 2 x 4s set on edge, are placed at two feet and eight feet apart within it. Light comes from bare bulbs strung on an X of bare wires tacked to the tent's four corner poles. Standing all around this pit, men hold their fingers up and call to each other, betting. Along the one side of the tent is a vast blackboard listing each contest, or hack, by name, weight and owner. All this smoke, light and racket meet and mingle in the tent's pinnacle like an oily storm cloud.

I went in by the drag pit; the small second pit used for matches that run-on too long with no victor, always a good way to enter a crowded pit tent. I've been to clandestine cockfighting clubs all over the southwest, but I had never seen anything like this. There must have been two hundred people milling about in and around this fighting arena.

An aisle was maintained clear from the main pit through the drag pit to the back door of the main house, which opened directly into the tent. Perpendicular to this door was the match scoreboard. Standing next to it holding an old school chalk eraser was my scrawny friend, Shake. But standing next to him was a surprise; a shock really: a woman, tall, lean and dark-eyed, and from hair to heel all in black; long shining jet black locks tumbled over a silken black blouse above a pencil skirt so tight it looked like she couldn't move. Her sharp boned cheeks were flawless and perfect and the way she flicked her cigarette ash off with the long nail of her thumb sent a chill through me that I couldn't fight off. I looked at Shake.

"Shake, you're the, the scorekeeper?" I asked haltingly while trying to steal glances at this stunning woman nearby, trying to take in her breathtaking presence. "But who the hell is that?" I whispered.

"Oh, hey Paul. Yeah, I'm keeping score. And, get this: I'm the bouncer, too!" Both of us laughed at this. Shake couldn't fight off an army of flies.

Wanting to be introduced to the woman behind him I tipped my head her way, but Shake almost imperceptibly shook his head 'no', then mouthed the words: 'devil's daughter.' Shake had a pint of bourbon and offered me the bottle.

"Everyone's trying to get past me into the house to get a look at Moffat's birds back in the coops." Shake spoke in a loud, stage voice, seemingly trying to impress the woman. They were both standing next to the door leading into the ranch house. "All the competing birds are in there caged up."

A longhaired fellow tried to push past Shake heading inside the house and coop, but Shake leaned across his path with a menacing smile. The kid forced a laugh and backed off.

"Where's Moffat?" I asked, after swigging. I tried to hand the bottle back to Shake, but the woman in black reached out and snapped it away. Twisting off the top, she pulled a long slow swig as we both watched, and then handed the empty bottle back to Shake, who took it and tossed it aside.

I didn't see the slap coming and neither did Shake. He took it though, which surprised me.

"I am not the 'devil's daughter' and if you say that again I will slap you again, little man." She looked over at me like I was buttered popcorn ready to be devoured. "I am Emiliana Elahefe."

Shake forced a laugh. "Yeah, this is Emiliana, Paul. Paul's a silversmith and stonecutter. He's a partner with Michael Atman, that fellow you just met inside with Moffat."

"Michael's in there?" I asked incredulously, pointing at the house.

"Yeah, he's in there with Moffat and her friends from Mexico. They're the only ones allowed in. Even Michael's not supposed to be in there, but he is. He's been drinking moonshine all week and he's tuned up tighter than a jigger's fiddle."

"Yeah, I know. Saw him earlier at the dance."

Emiliana hadn't taken her eyes off me. "I don't like your partner," she said, finally, a predator's smile fixed upon her face.

"He's not my partner anymore."

"Good," she said. "Then you won't mind if I say terrible things about him."

"I didn't say that; he's still my friend." Her smile vanished like the Cheshire cat's.

There was a beer bar set up at the other end of the tent so I nodded at it. "Let's go get a beer, Shake. Nice to meet you, ma'am," I said to her. Then we moved away from this smoking woman in black. Her eyes followed us with deep disdain as we retreated.

"Are you going to bet, Paul?" Shake asked as we walked over. "If you are, I'll wanna let you in on the big secret. I owe you one for that work you threw me."

I was curious about other things. "Who is that woman?" I asked as soon as we were out of earshot.

"Don't ask me, 'cause you don't want to know."

"What do you mean?"

"She brought Moffat up a ringer from old Mexico." He spoke in a low voice. At the bar, we both ordered up drafts.

"What do you mean?" I kept one eye on Shake and one eye on Emiliana across the room. She cast a malevolent grin my way and I shuddered inside like a child. Not sure why.

"The eighth hack is Moffat against Mr. Mero's bird. He's that professional Mexican fighter that followed us up from town. Mero doesn't expect any trouble. His bird's a two-time winner. Big Brady-Roundhead; badass bird and pit-wise too. So the odds are currently ten to one against Moffat's bird."

"So you're telling me Mero's bird is the bet in the eighth match?" I asked, pushing him to the point. Emiliana was still eyeing us both suspiciously, as she should have been, since Shake was about to betray Moffat. I couldn't keep my eyes off her. It was like looking at raw, unadulterated danger.

"No, no, no. That's just it...Emiliana..." Shake tipped his head back over his own shoulder ever so slightly towards her, "...brought up this beautiful Spanish Cross from the finest Ranchero in all Mexico. Apparently, she's some champion cock fighter's daughter—a wild child. And this bird she sold Moffat is just a total killer! Four-time winner in Mexico. You should see him! Head's all dubbed down, comb as red a fire engine. Just this really game bird."

As we sipped our beers, Shake produced another flat bottle of Old Grand Dad from his back pocket and we again traded shots. The sound of a sudden, violent crowing and a furious flapping of wings suddenly came from within the house.

"That bird just storms around in there," Shake cackled.

Emiliana turned to the house door and called out some guttural sound from deep in her throat. It might have been in Spanish, but I really couldn't tell. It was just a screeching sound to me. Instantly, the bird inside fell silent.

"So lay some money on Solomon!" Shake insisted.

"Bird's name is Solomon?" I asked. "You're kidding, right?"

"No, that's what Moffat calls him. Says he'll split Mero's bird right down the middle. You should lay some money on him before Mero wises up."

"Who is taking bets?"

"Pretty much everybody, all the handlers for sure. And there's a guy they call Broadmoor Bill who'll take any bet." Shake pointed across the pit. "The guy with the white skimmer." Shake began whispering again. "But whatever you do, don't tell anyone about Solomon."

"Listen, Shake, I want to make some bets, but I'd like to come back and watch from the scoreboard with you. Good view of the pit. Save me a spot?"

"Sure. I get the whole area for working the board. Better hurry though. First pitting is in ten minutes, and after that, the odds will go down."

As I was leaving, I saw two men come out of the house behind Emiliana. They were both heavyset, wearing loud Hawaiian shirts and speaking rapidly in Spanish. Shake turned as he walked away and winked at me, "Mexico," he mouthed.

The two men joined Emiliana and all three had a loud conference in Spanish. Then I saw a bankroll come out of one of the men's pockets. It was huge. He went out into the crowd to place their bets with Broadmoor Bill. I followed him.

The smoke was twice as thick outside of the pit area. Broadmoor Bill was taking bets in classic cockfight style. Right hand holding all the money between each finger and a pad strapped to his left wrist, on which he wrote down each bet with a small pencil. I noticed what appeared to be two bodyguards hovering in the background protecting him. Just as I was about to bet, I saw Mr. Mero signaling me from the near corner of the tent. Coming up to him, he beckoned for me to follow him outside to where his car was parked.

"Good evening, Paul." He shook my hand very formally. "I wish to speak with you on a very delicate matter. Although you appear to have no formal connection with Senor Moffat, I should ask you not to repeat what I will say to you, before I say it."

"Sure, Mr. Mero, I won't say a word of anything you tell me. But I must tell you that I will not reveal anything that I have been told in confidence."

"Si. Paul, this is why I like you. You have honor and have been a gentleman this last week. This, I admire. Now listen carefully. My hack with Senor Moffat: I just wish to say that I have more than one bird that weighs 5:02 and the contest rules say I can fight any one of them." He paused, and reaching around to his back pocket he pulled out the smallest silver flask I had ever seen.

"Mescal," he said, tilting the flask at me. I nodded, and he poured a small amount into the tiny cup top and handed it to me. It was ornately carved and pure silver. Here was a man with a sense of elegance. I took the shot.

"And that any smart man," he continued, "could wait 'til the fight begins, 'til a point when everyone sees the power of Moffat's bird and the odds go against my bird. Then he bets on me."

He smiled brightly, and then took a swallow of mescal. Carefully replacing the top, he hipped the flask.

"You see, Paul, my 5:02 would not be the bird they are expecting. I have another who is more ring-wise, who loves to fight young birds. I have trained him to take the first pittings defensively. I know this is dangerous, but the bird seems to like it and it is very good for betting."

"Thank you for sharing this with me. Puedo hablar español si prefieres," I said.

"Oh, si." He was delighted to speak in Spanish. "Esto es magnífico. Pero tengo miedo de que haya muchas cosas para preparar la competición. Podemos hablar después, pero recuerda lo que te ha dicho."

He went around to the side of his car and brought out his gaff case.

"Mucha suerte, Enrique, y muchas gracias.

"Yes, yes," he winked, waving me away. Then he sat down on the running board of his car, opened his case and began removing the razor sharp gaffs.

Broadmoor Bill took a few small bets from me. Just tens and twenties on birds whose owners' names I recognized. I decided to take Mr. Mero's advice and wait on the eighth hack.

Making my way to Shake's scoreboard, I noticed that Emiliana was gone. As I arrived, the first cock emerged from the house door. The owner/handler was holding the bird by the crook beneath his wings, and the bird was crowing and screeching. He was bright red with black ends to his tight, robust feathers. Glinting on the cock's legs were the pointed, rod-like, razor sharp gaffs.

Seeing the first bird come out the crowd got louder than ever. This first handler went around the side of the pit and stopped before the judge and referee. I was stunned.

Emiliana had moved over and taken a position next to the Judge. Emiliana was going to be the referee!

She carefully and expertly examined the bird and the gaffs. They were fighting short spurs so she made sure they were properly and solidly placed. After a moment, she nodded to the judge, and the bird's handler went over to the far score within the pit to wait for his challenger.

Getting a signal from Emiliana, Shake opened the door to the house and the second fighting cock came out in his handler's arms. This bird was black and speckled and crowing even more fiercely than his opponent. Once again, the dull, grey glint of blades caught my eye. Moffat followed this handler out and gave me the briefest of glances as he passed the scoreboard.

This second pair wound around the pit to the same position in the front of the judge and Emiliana. Again, she examined this bird and the spurs strapped to his legs. Again, she nodded to the judge and this second handler took a position on the other set of scores.

With a mere swirl of her hand the woman reined the noisy, smoking tent into silence. All eyes went to her. Expertly, with only the slightest lift of her sharp-boned chin she shifted the attention to the judge, who was standing pit side. Calling out in a voice that all could hear he announced: "Welcome to the Mountain Party Invitational. This is the first pitting of the first match in a multiple pitting contest. Short spurs. Contestants." He pointed to the first bird. "Sam the First handled by his owner Matt Taylor, vs. Jeff Beck handled by Andy Dylon, and owned by our host, Mr. Roger Moffat."

"Now bill them!" shouted the woman in a thick Spanish accent. With this she waved the handlers into the center where they began shoving the birds at each other to make them angry. Both birds began to shriek in rage. The crowd joined in screaming for the contest to finally begin, screaming for warfare, screaming for blood. With a vertical slicing movement of her arms Emiliana signaled the handlers to step back.

That's when it happened. Right in front of all of us: somehow Emiliana seemed to change her form into that of a stalking mountain lion; a black shadow of threat moving counter-clockwise around the ring; death itself stalking the pit like a sensual tango dancer.

She seemed to be intimidating both the birds and their handlers. The handlers were as stunned as the crowd and didn't know what to do.

Then, stopping as abruptly as she had started, she opened her long arms and hands out wide, drumming her long slender fingers in the air, her talon-like fingernails flashing in the harsh light of the bare bulbs above. Again, the entire crowd fell silent, birds included, all drawn to watching her fingertips in the dusty light and simultaneously falling under her ominous spell. Throwing her long, wavy, black mane of hair back in a curl like a snapping whip, she let out another guttural cry that seemed to ripple the very walls of the tent,

"¡A la muerte! Empezar!"

No one moved. Pounding my back brain for my feeble grade school Spanish, it finally came to me: "To the death! Let us begin!" The crowd roared its approval.

Then Emiliana waved the two handlers into the inner pit. "Birds will be dropped at the count of three." She paused again for silence and got it instantly.

"One, two, three: drop!" Emiliana stepped backed quickly away as the birds were released. A flash of steel passing in front of her eyes as the two birds flew at each other in attack. But Moffat's bird, Jeff Beck, had gotten the better of the drop. Wings wide, he glided down on top of Sam and in one movement, entangled his claws in Sam's leather protective breastplate. But Jeff Beck was unable to get the killing stroke in.

Both birds fell over, each holding fast to the other. Emiliana signaled the handlers in. Being grabbed, both cocks instinctively let go of their death grasp. No nursing was required, and Sam's breastplate had not been pierced, so Emiliana again signaled for quiet, and the second drop began.

This time, both birds dropped straight down and did not engage. Instead, they circled in an ever-tightening pattern, heads low and screeching fiercely. Just before their circling encounter was about to end, Jeff Beck flew up in front of the startled Sam, and drove his gaff home into the claret's neck. Both birds went over, Sam dead instantly, with Jeff Beck still attached to its side because his spur had hit bone.

"¡A la Muerte!" Emiliana called to the judge. Some of the men looked at her differently now. What had been fascinating was now frightening. The judge signaled Shake which was the losing bird with a finger pulled across his throat and with a tiny squeaky piece of chalk, Shake wrote up Jeff Beck's victory on the scoreboard. The bettors went wild. I looked for Moffat's reaction: just the faintest of smiles.

Matt Taylor went out and helped Andy get Jeff Beck free. Then he took his bird's corpse quietly out through the drag pit. Shake leaned over, "I won seventy-five dollars," he smiled.

"Not a bad start."

"Did you win?"

"Didn't bet. Didn't know the birds."

"Well I can tell ya, Moffat's birds are gonna sweep. They're all meaner than hell." Shake was drunk. Not a lot, but for him, a little.

"Okay, Shake, maybe next time. When's Moffat's next hack?"

"That's it! His next one's not 'til the eighth and I already told you about that!" He put his arm around me. "You be sure and put some money on Solomon, I told you now." He slapped me on the back.

"Don't you tell him nothing!" It was Michael coming up out of the house behind us. Wild-eyed and robust, his bullet-black eyes fell on Emiliana. Licking his lips, he looked her straight in the eye then blew her a kiss. This made her furious.

"¡A la muerte!" she shrieked at him.

Turning back to Shake and me, Michael said: "Shake, if you talk to that traitor I'll skin you like a beaver!" To emphasize this point, he grabbed Shake around the shoulder and dragged him along with him as he pushed past me.

He hauled Shake, with his arm tight across his back, the ten yards to the tent's entrance where he let him go suddenly, dropping him like a sack, without breaking stride. Shake couldn't get to his feet, and stumbled and fell. A few fellows nearby picked him up. Michael never looked back as he left the tent. Still furious, Emiliana followed him out and a new fellow stepped up to referee the next match.

"He's a mean drunk," said Shake as he came up beside me at the scoreboard. "It's night or day with him. He's a completely different dude when he's drunk. I swear, he even gets stronger. It's diabolical." Falling had sobered Shake up and he grew angry now. "I'm gonna get that bastard one day when he's not looking."

"Really?" I asked. Shake stopped dusting himself off and looked at me. "You won't tell him I said that?" asked Shake, nervously.

"No. I won't say a word," I answered over my shoulder as I headed out for some fresh air.

CHAPTER XV

A mountain night, with the wide, starry stripe of the Milky Way splitting the night sky like a tiara; a shimmering silver moon plays magnificent monarch in a cradle of regal clouds. Below, weak, slaking campfires dot the meadow, reflecting the stars above. All activity has now diminished down to that going on inside the tent attached to the bark-patched Moffat ranch house. But with its flaps rolled down, this activity is now sealed inside canvas walls. When the flap opens, a triangle of lantern light, and a cloud of dense blue smoke are expelled out into the night air. A constant ruckus, sometimes human and sometimes rooster, leaks out of this tent like the cacophony of some jazz music. Through the ranch house windows solemn men rove about taking birds out of wire coops and conveying them

out of the cabin and into the fighting tent. There,
the human horde suddenly roars its approval as one
bird falls to his challenger and dies.

It was a mild night, so I stayed outside for a long while. I could tell by the moisture in the air that rain was coming. The wind was making a lot of noise among the trees along the western edge of the pasture. The noise attracted my attention, so I went over there and walked among the rustling trees for a while. It was restful for my spirit. There were no branches on the trees for the first twenty feet up, so it seemed as though I was walking under a high green canopy.

I heard them before I saw them, grunting and moaning. It took me a while to recognize what I was hearing and by then I was already upon them, terribly embarrassed because I saw what they were doing, before I could stop.

It was Michael and Emiliana. He had her up against a tree trunk with her legs wrapped around his still denim clad butt. He heard my approach and turned to see who it was. We locked eyes.

Emiliana saw me too, but neither of them stopped or said anything. I backed up quickly, spun around, and hustled off in a different direction.

The interim cockfights didn't interest me, but I definitely wanted to see the eighth hack so I just kept walking in the moonlight, trying to forget what I had just seen.

I must have walked around for quite a while because when I got back to the tent they were just preparing for the eighth match. I shouldered up to Shake once again and he seemed genuinely glad to see me. The air was smokier than before, and there were no women fans left in the crowd, except the now-returned Emiliana. The roar of the crowd never seemed to drop below a certain roaring level.

"Hey Paul, I got some cold Olympia stashed. You want one?" Shake didn't wait for a reply, but went off behind the scoreboard. Returning, he handed me a sweating can. The cold beer tasted great at that late hour. I had more or less decided on my walk that I wasn't going to drink hard liquor anymore that night, so the beer was a welcome slake for my thirst.

Far off across the arena, I could see Michael swaggering about, people carefully moving out of his way. I watched as he suddenly rounded up in the far corner and headed straight toward Broadmoor Bill. Remembering what Enrique had told me, and had made me promise, I figured it would be all right if I just hinted to Michael not to bet on Solomon. I mean, I wouldn't tell him why. We'd been partners, once.

"Back in a bit, Shake."

Dodging through the crowd, I intercepted Michael a few feet from the bookie.

"Michael, hang on there. I gotta talk to you." I steered him towards the corner of the tent.

"What the hell do you want?" He was loud.

"Listen, I won't waste time. You're an old friend. I know you think you're in for a big killing, but I got a clue for you. Hold your bet."

"What are you talkin' about? Something Shake told you? Don't need either of you to tell me how to bet. And I especially don't need to know anything *you* might want to tell me. As a matter of fact..."

Michael made a grab for my shirt collar, but I jumped back away in time. I could feel the wind from his arm swiping the air in front of me as it went past.

"What a piece of work you are, you little turd. I think all of us on earth have pretty much gotten all the use out of you we are gonna get." He spat on the ground between us. His eyes were ringed-red. He seemed about to spit in my face. I just stood there.

Within the tent, the noise of the crowd rose to a new crescendo as Emiliana again took up her position as the ref. At ringside the judge stepped up to announce the eighth pitting.

"Out of my way," Michael told me, "I'm betting on this match." And he walked off towards Broadmoor Bill. I went back to join Shake at the scoreboard.

From there I saw Enrique come in and approach the pit. He set up a folding chair, and a small suitcase with legs that folded out to make it into a table. He went out again and returned cradling his bird. The crowd watched, intensely fascinated.

Unlike the other cocks, Mr. Mero's bird was completely silent. Enrique sat down in the chair and began to prepare him. Most of the other fighters did this behind closed doors, so a small group of bettors and gawkers formed directly behind him to watch. I noticed a couple of Moffat's pals paying particular attention. I figured Moffat was still inside the cabin readying Solomon.

Enrique took his time, removing the tools from his case and carefully applying alcohol and chamois to the bird's low-stationed heels. I could see that they were again fighting short spurs.

No matter what Enrique did, the bird never spooked, moved erratically or screeched. A lot of the longhaired fellows watching from behind seemed to be pretty amazed by this. Enrique never looked up until Broadmoor Bill made a pass on him. Then he looked straight up at him, fiercely in the eye, and the bookie just kept on walking.

"Enrique doesn't seem to like Bill very much," said Shake. He had been watching, too.

"No, he doesn't," I said. "Or maybe he just doesn't like Bill's odds. He can't make any money favored 5-1."

I knew otherwise, of course, but I was honor bound not to say. Shake laughed and agreed.

A new screeching rose up from the coops in the house behind us, and in a moment, the door was kicked open. Moffat's best handler, Andy Dylon, emerged carrying the most beautiful cockfighting bird I had ever seen; white, but dramatically speckled red, and atop his crown a bright red and rigid comb. As soon as he came out, the bird realized he was going to face, so he started crowing and screeching like a banshee. The mob started crowing along with him and for the full minute it took Dylon and Moffat to make their way around the pit, you couldn't hear anything but that sound. I looked over at Enrique. He didn't even raise his head.

Andy Dylon, with Moffat beside him, presented Solomon to Emiliana for examination. Emiliana took her time, but after a moment, nodded to the judge and indicated to Dylon to take the far set of scores. Then, she turned to Enrique, and called for his bird. Enrique did not look up or say anything, but raised one finger high to indicate he'd be ready in one moment. The whole crowd quieted during this moment. Then Enrique rose slowly and approached Emiliana.

Even though Solomon was taunting him as he was carried over, Enrique's bird still made no sound. I remembered what Enrique had said about the bird being pit-wise.

While Emiliana checked the gaffs on Enrique's bird the judge asked the cock's name and weight.

"His name is Mero, and his weight is 5:02."

Emiliana handed the bird back and pointed for Enrique to take his place at the other set of scores. The match was about to start. I figured it was time to find Broadmoor Bill so I could make my bet once the odds changed. Looking around, I spotted his big, white cowboy hat sticking up out of the crowd. He was about twenty feet away and easily within hollering distance. The judge called out from the side of the ring:

"Eighth hack. Five pounds, two ounces, Solomon vs. Mero. Solomon is handled by Andy Dylon, and owned by our host Roger Moffat. Mero is owned and handled by Mr. Enrique." Emiliana paused and looked over at Enrique. "¿Qué es su nombre?" she asked.

"Mero," replied Enrique with a small smile.

"Mero is owned and handled by Enrique Mero." Again with a graceful movement of her arm Emiliana signaled the handlers into the pit. "Now bill your birds, hombres."

Emiliana stepped out and the handlers approached each other with their birds held out at arm's length. Instantaneously, Enrique's bird came to life. He almost escaped Enrique's grasp as he leaped out towards the other cock, screeching with fury. "That's enough," called Emiliana, and again with a slicing movement of her arms she signaled the handlers back.

Then it happened again. Emiliana began to stalk around the pit in a menacing circle, sometimes facing the fighters and sometimes facing out towards the bloodthirsty crowd. This time the crowd was completely seduced. They cheered and whistled at her erotic dance before death.

Taking up her original position, Emiliana then ripped her black scarf from around her neck and, putting it in her mouth, she tore it in half, corner to corner, using her teeth. Then she flung out her long arms and threw both pieces of fabric up into the air. The two gauzy pieces floated slowly back to earth each one landing beside one of the handlers, who looked up at her, puzzled, but intrigued.

The crowd began to chant. "Emiliana, Emiliana, Emiliana."

Reaching her arms out wide again, her glistening, ringed fingers once more drummed the smoky air and slowly, so slowly, she swayed her hips. Again, the crowd fell perfectly silent, all eyes on her sultry hip movements in the dim light of this place that now smelled of blood. Finally, throwing her hair back and forth and side to side in a ferocious wave, she let out her guttural call to start:

"¡A la muerte! Empezar!"

The place went nuts. Pretty much everyone there was drunk by now and they loved it. People threw full glasses of beer at each other. Fights broke out between friends. Broadmoor Bill's guards stepped up immediately to shield him from the mayhem.

Horrified, Emiliana screamed at the top of her voice: "¡Ya basta!" A screech not unlike the screech of one of the birds.

The rioting stopped at once. She slowly looked around at the men and a new, more lasting, calm settled in. Once this was achieved she turned her attention back to the pit. Flicking her wrists at the two handlers, they stepped quickly up to their scores.

"First pitting on three." Emiliana called out, then she yelled: "One, two, three, drop!"

Hackles raised high, the two cocks went straight after each other. Solomon got the advantage of the drop and shuffled over the top of Mero. But using his speed, Mero escaped from underneath and circled away to fight again. The two birds now closed in to a tight circular pattern keeping their heads low.

Then Solomon leaped. Once again, Mero escaped by running underneath the airborne cock. I could almost feel the odds dropping. Obviously, Solomon was a killer.

As soon as Solomon landed, he turned back and was off again. This time, Mero didn't have time to run. Instead, he deflected the deathblow with his wing. Solomon's gaff became entangled in the other bird's wing spindles and was unable to strike Mero with his free spur.

"Handle!" called out Emiliana. The handlers went in and carefully separated the two birds. They had thirty seconds to nurse, but Enrique ignored Mero's wing. Apparently, there was no real damage or blood drawn. Both men held their bird's faces up to their own and blew air rapidly down into their throats to revive them.

"Second pitting!" called Emiliana.

I decided to make my way over to Broadmoor Bill, and was standing almost next to him when the second drop began. Once again, Solomon got the advantage, fighting aerial, he raked over Mero's eyes with his claws, but was unable to get the spur in. Solomon did cut the other bird's dub, but the wounds were superficial, still no blood. Mero, reacting ferociously leapt up and drove Solomon back. Both birds landed apart and began to circle again.

By this time the crowd had realized that their host had fooled them. That Moffat had a ringer. Broadmoor Bill was swamped with people trying to reverse their five or ten to one bets *against* Solomon.

Coming close to Broadmoor Bill's ear I yelled, "I'll take Mero, twenty to one, five hundred dollars."

Broadmoor Bill looked at me like I was his guardian angel.

"You want five hundred on Mero at twenty to one?" he yelled. I guess he thought I was crazy, I don't know. There were a lot of people yelling at him to bet the other way, so he probably thought he might as well cover. I nodded that this was my bet.

"I'll take it at ten to one," he said.

I nodded and he instantly wrote it down on his wrist pad, tore it off and handed it to me. I gave him my five hundred dollars. All I had. He kept taking bets, all on Solomon, so I snaked back through the crowd to the scoreboard and Shake.

The birds had become entangled again while I was betting, and the handlers had separated the birds and taken them out of the pit.

Enrique was rough nursing Mero by briskly rubbing the cock's neck. The bird screeched and seemed to enjoy it. I could see Moffat standing behind Andy who was handling Solomon on the far side of the ring. By Moffat's smirk, I could tell he thought victory was in hand. In seconds Emiliana indicated time for the third pitting.

Just before the third drop, I saw Enrique give Mero a squeeze, which is just this side of legal. The bird reacted like a demon. Solomon again took to the air, but instead of having a stationary target at which to aim, Mero was also airborne. The birds met about three feet off the ground in dead center ring. They flailed and slashed, but neither could strike a death-blow. Mero did cut the cross's breastplate, but only superficially.

Both birds landed and Mero attacked again, fiercely. The crowd quieted, realizing the change of fates. Mero swept in low with his head down. As he came close, Solomon brought his beak down on Mero's neck, cutting it, but not opening it up, still no blood. Throwing his head back, Mero knocked Solomon off his feet.

Mero was on him in a second and drove his spur straight through the cross's neck. At almost the same time, Solomon was driving a gaff deep into Mero's under-cage. They both fell over and within a minute both were dead.

Nobody knew who had won. Enrique and Andy both went out and separated their birds. Emiliana went over to the Judge and they talked through cupped hands in each other's ears.

Then, Emiliana nodded to the judge and went back into the center of the ring. Each handler stood on their scores, cradling their dead birds.

"Eighth hack, both cocks killed, the winner is decided by first blood: Mero, owned by Enrique Mero."

Since most folks had switched their bets to Solomon during the match, there was a lot of angry yelling and screaming.

Moffat didn't hesitate for a moment. He walked directly out into the ring, took a knife from his belt sheath, and cut Solomon's head off. Then he turned around and threw it in front of the judge. This was the ultimate insult. The screaming doubled, and the ring was showered with coins from the angry losers. Emiliana was the angriest of all. She spat onto Moffat's back as he walked away.

Enrique stood tall at five feet amid this onslaught. He left the ring and exited through the drag pit, heading out to the previously dug out open grave where he would lay his namesake among the others.

On the way out, I caught his eye. He dropped his poker face and winked at me. I nodded and smiled, letting him know I had taken his advice. He continued out. I wasn't worried about collecting my five-thousand dollars, cockfighting and the betting around it is game of honor, so I knew Broadmoor Bill would be there whenever I got to him.

Disgusted, Moffat and Dylon exited into the cabin, disrespectfully leaving Solomon's headless carcass behind at the score. Emiliana kicked a hole in the soft ground with her heel and slid Solomon's head in. Then she came over to the scoreboard and taking Shake's chalk-stick, she put a line through Moffat's name wherever it appeared. This disqualified Moffat from the tournament, and probably from fighting anywhere in the southwest. Word gets around quickly in cockfighting. There was more to Emiliana then met the eye.

After a few minutes, things had quieted down, and they were ready for the ninth hack. I decided to collect my money and go back up to camp. It was getting light, and I was tired. I had seen the match I wanted to see.

Broadmoor Bill was just outside the tent with his two bodyguards. He was busy paying off and collecting debts, but mostly paying. He stopped when he saw me. He didn't say anything, but reached out his hand for my bet receipt. I gave it to him, he read it, and looked up at me and smiled a slow, wide, smile.

"Good bet,'" he said.

The other fellows around us quieted as they watched him count out my money. Most of them were paying off, so they probably felt pretty bad seeing my winnings. But nobody bothered me or said anything until Bill was finished and I turned to go.

The punch came out of nowhere. It hit me in the stomach, and doubled me over. The bodyguards got a firm hold of Michael before he could swing again. It took both of them to hold him.

"You son of a bitch!" Michael yelled. "That's my money. You and that Mexican had it all figured, you bastard. This'll be the last time you make a fool out of me. I want your ass up the hill right now."

The punch had both hurt me and made me angry. I had had enough, too. Emiliana screaming 'A la muerte' was still ringing in my ears. Some things are worth fighting for, dying for even, and for me, love was one of them.

"Let him go," I said. "He's going to get exactly what he wants this morning."

The bookie's bodyguards let him go, and he spun around and away. I put the wads of bills in my pocket, and followed him up and away from the gathering.

Chapter XVI

A clear-cut circle, sizeable and round and slanted east on the face of Moffat's otherwise thickly timbered mountain; a perfectly round bare patch surrounded by musically swaying pines, and within which the only fresh growth are luminous white mushrooms, popping like puffy marshmallows from raw, bark stripped stumps. The cold, eastern wind increases, bringing in a solid bank of sky-slicing clouds, veined black with rain. The moon is briefly completely obscured by this new front and all light is lost. A sad grayness is cast upon the range from the hidden sun. Within this clear-cut ring, droplets sputter among the pinecones, leaves and dead needles as it begins to rain. Along the lower perimeter, two men scuttle into this circular timber harvest, the first one hustling to keep uphill of the other.

My heart pounded hard as I followed Michael up and away from the tent and the camping meadow where I knew Sarah and Stuart lay sleeping.

After we left the soft grass of the meadow, the ground grew harder the higher we went. Once we entered the forest I had to wade through thick layers of dead aspen leaves. Others times there were wide-open paths of aged and almost silent pine needles.

Then I noticed the trees grew straighter and taller. The whole forest had turned into lumber grade Douglas fir. This is the same timber you buy in your lumberyard and Moffat had a forest of it; thick straight fir trees that would mill out well and produce lots of unknotted board feet. Michael pushed on and I could see he was making for some sort of clearing ahead.

Waves of questions washed over me as I strained to keep up with Michael. Why was I here? What did I have to prove? Where did this pleasurable sense of impending violence come from? I suddenly realized I was absolutely furious with Michael, raging angry at his stubborn bull-headedness, but that I also loved him like a brother. It was a terrible and confusing mix of feelings.

Suddenly the continuous flow of evergreens all around me stopped and I was in a wide clearing. Around me was a huge clear-cut circle with a tall, bark-stripped, tree at its center with giant chains and other logging gear hanging from its top like a medieval war machine.

Michael's body seemed to tick as I followed him into this huge hollowed-out area of the woods. His head was always on the swivel, looking for any peril from any direction, any other unwanted people on the scene. But I could also see that his nerves were barely under control. Twice, I saw his right arm leap away from him in what appeared to be an involuntary action.

Above me on the mountainside, Michael leaped and dashed about, appearing and disappearing inside this giant circle of stumps; his flannel shirt would appear and then disappear amidst the short straight shadows of the giant roots left behind by the axe men.

Michael had headed north straight from the scuffle outside the cockfighting tent; heading directly for this bald spot in the lush green forest. An eyesore that everyone in the meadow had observed and talked about over the last few days. Many called it a scar on the land. Moffat had sold the trees to finance his high lifestyle. Some folks had actually left once they realized the money for the party had come directly from the killing of those trees.

From the perimeter of this treeless circle I could see it was about a quarter-mile across. Michael wanted plenty of room and privacy.

Michael looked sharp staying ahead of me. He was in good shape but had done a lot of drinking. I could hear his strained breathing.

He wanted to choose the exact location of our fight. He was a soldier and wanted to choose his ground. This was a special fight, one he had been waiting for, one he planned to win.

I suddenly realized that this was more than just a fight, this was a duel. It was dawn. It was raining. He had unknown intentions. Was this going to be a fight to the death? Was that too outrageous to think? What was about to occur between Michael and me? Or would anything happen at all?

And then another thought sobered me. We had never had a duel before, just fights and arguments and wrestling matches. But this time I knew Michael wanted vengeance for more than just the current angry void between us about a stupid cockfight. This time was very different and there was a lot more at stake than had ever been at stake before. And that scared me.

Michael still hiked above me. After a few more leaping steps I saw him stop beside the tree in the center of this bald circle of stumps. I stopped too and took in a three hundred and sixty degree view of his position. In a second, I realized exactly where Michael was standing.

He was, as near as I could tell, positioned in the exact center of this timber emptiness: the gladiator position in this log-strewn arena.

The rain gradually slowed to a drizzle. After catching my breath, for I didn't want to arrive out of breath, I hiked up to where Michael was standing. He never took his eyes off me. Even from this distance I could still see that his stance was one I had seen a hundred times before; arms taut, fists clenched, ready for anything. But, before now, I had always seen him like this from the side, when we were fighting someone else together.

Now, I was his adversary, and for the first time I saw the predator in his eyes. His arms hung low along his sides, muscles bulging, his fists continually clenching and unclenching.

I stopped just below him in this grim, man-made clearing, about ten feet away. Casually lifting one foot up I placed it on a stump, asking:

"What do you want?"

"You know Paul, there are two kinds of worms, those who slither and those who crawl. But both eat dirt and shove it out the back. Just like you. You eat my dirt and shove it out the back. I'm giving you fair warning. This is it; my time, my place, my moment. This morning I get even and give you the beating of your life."

"Why? For what? Because Enrique's bird killed yours? Because Sarah loves me? Because you're deaf to the entire world? Or is it simply because everyone else has to suffer because of your unresolved Viet Nam madness?"

That was more than enough. By the time I got the word "madness" out, he was already on the attack, on his way for me. He covered the distance between us quickly, his anger fueling his muscles with a charge of adrenaline.

Just as he came within range I drew my fist back and lunging out, I smashed his face as hard as I could. Even though I had hit him solidly in the face somehow the soldier in him still came straight on at me and never stopped. He tackled me hard, knocking me backward then used his head to butt my forehead. I found myself bent painfully backwards over a stump. I don't know whose it was, but there was blood everywhere.

We kicked off the stump locked together like rabid alligators and rolled around on that dead forest floor, smacking hard into tree stumps, one after the other.

Michael's screaming and swearing was a full throttle rage: bubbling red, furious-faced, mad-dog, ruptured rib-cage rage. And, for the first time in all the times we'd fought, he bit me, a quick hard, vicious bite that punctured my forearm.

Then, like the striking of a red top match on an iron stove, my own fury suddenly flared in a flame and I hit him back as hard as I could in the face. His own violence had ignited my temper and now I completely let go. Seeing an opening I kneed him hard in the balls, and he fell completely over backward instantly, stunned and moaning.

My nose was broken and bleeding from his original head butt, but I could still see. My mouth gasped for air in short breaths. Somehow, I stood up.

He rose with me. "You took Sarah away," he screeched, "You took Sarah away from me, you little bastard!"

"That's a lie. You know your own guilt forced her away. And you know what else? I know all about it!" I shrieked back, right up in his face, all my composure gone.

He feigned a move away, then came back at me with a strong jab, ever the strategic soldier. He swung this punch fiercely, but I already knew from past tangles with Michael that you had to stay out of the way of his jabs, and this time I was quicker then ever before. I dodged his jab entirely and infuriated, head to toe, with my heart pounding, instead of backing off, I went in tight against him and flurried back rock hard punches, straight into his face. Beating him up.

Michael toppled back.

"Yeah, Michael, I know why you came back from 'Nam and why you took up with Sarah. You had to replace the man you shot and killed yourself. You had to replace your partner, Drummond!" I was worked up, really ready to knock him off his perch. "And now you've got me cast as some kind of understudy! But you cannot make it work; too much guilt I figure, pulling that trigger and all. So you chose me as the man to replace Drummond in Sarah's life."

His face suddenly dissolved to no countenance at all, no affect, no face contours of any kind; an empty slate, all human thought gone. An animalistic killing machine now had taken over. His face took on the flickering raw features of an open flame. He instantly savagely re-attacked me, his fury now doubled, a possessed demon out for death.

Jumping on top of me, Michael's strong hands latched around my neck in a vise grip, his thumbs pressing into my throat and voice box so I couldn't speak. But I knew what he was doing. It was a choking death grip.

On my back, with Michael on top of me my vision went almost pure white and I couldn't breathe at all. Michael's eyes stood out in this strange almost unconscious void with no skull attached.

Then, behind his socket-less eyes, a stump appeared to my right. Gauging the distance to it, I rolled over toward it as hard as I could, turning us both twice.

Then, on the high side of the second roll, I threw all my weight on top of Michael so that his skull struck the trunk directly and hard. His eyes looked very startled, then reddened, then closed like a fire curtain. He was unconscious.

Off him, I crawled away to the shelter of another stump, a good fifteen feet away, and I just lay there. My windpipe ached and my throat felt as thin as a pencil.

So, I thought to myself, this was the peak of Michael's world: a torturous violence composed of rage, hatred and death.

It was many minutes before I felt well enough to try and pull myself up to sit on top of the stump that was sheltering me from the soft rain. The air seemed much clearer and fresher there, and I looked over to where my friend lay. I hoped Michael wasn't dead, and part of me didn't care.

The rain freshened with the rise of the sun, with plumb clear droplets the size of your thumb. My shirt and jeans were soaking wet and mud-caked, but I felt no discomfort. I was numb, but okay and satisfied that things were finally settled, sort of. My nose felt like a pig's snout whenever I touched it.

Soon the rain roused Michael. But he wasn't better. He was much worse.

Slowly he stood up, shaking his head to clear it. Then he saw me and just stared, smiling slowly, but still looking very much like a broken, pathetic man, alone in the world, but now seemingly happy again to be able to destroy something beautiful.

"Michael," I said, quietly, finding my voice hoarse but calm, "I found your combat journal. I read it, Michael. I read the last entry. I know all about you and Stuart's father, Drummond. And it doesn't matter"

"YOU TOLD HER!" he screeched, his voice breaking and his face melting into disbelief and panic.

I didn't move from my seat. "No, Michael. I didn't. I didn't tell Sarah because it's not for me to tell her anything about this. I cannot do it. It's for you to do, and only if you think it's right. But you must see what not telling her has done to you. The things you've said and done. How you've protected her, then shoved her away. How you've taken this all out on me. Michael, I know about it all. Do you understand? Someone else knows the whole story of what happened in Viet Nam, and I understand."

His face softened and a million cracks and crevices suddenly appeared in his woebegone, sad face. Shocked, I was stunned to see a streak of gray had woven a wave through his stringy, damp hair. He was aging before my eyes.

"I understand, too," Michael said, choking, and I watched his hand snake around his back. A snap opened and his hand emerged with his knife.

I never believed it possible, but now, in this high wilderness timber clear-cut, there was something I had never seen before in my former partner's eyes: murder. I rose quickly from my stump, adrenaline pumping into my veins as I rose, unsheathed my own blade, and backed away from him.

But as he approached, I remembered another clearing, a clearing not in my life, but in his. A far away jungle clearing that he fought in a long, long time ago. A clearing he had never really left behind.

And I thought, 'Here is my best friend. My finest, and most loyal friend, even if there are occasional fisticuffs, here he is out of his mind with a toxic dose of long-held, misplaced guilt: a killing in the past that so devastated him that he is willing to commit a murder in the present to cover it up. Madness.'

Michael's brain had wrapped up all his hideous feelings about killing Drummond and carefully bound them within a thick olive-drab elastic band. Then he carefully stashed those files away in a desolate corner of his own mind; a high, windswept desert part of himself that was filled only with a million grains of guilt, a rough Old Testament justice, and broken friendships scattered around like browned, dead cacti.

The blood-dripping murder of Drummond, in every technical and sensual detail, still resided in that cobwebbed corner of Michael's worn and weary mind.

Drink and drugs had soothed and smoothed things out for him for eons, but no substance or treatment could ever make his guilt go away completely. Only the love of a sincere and honest relationship could heal him to the core, and with his own behavior that was highly unlikely to ever actually happen. His illness doomed him to be, and remain, alone.

I knew that terrible truths about what Michael had done to other human beings in Viet Nam were all still right there, just below the surface, and held together by an elastic band called an Honorable Discharge.

But right now, Michael's soul was too far out, stretched thin as the skin of a snare drum, poised to snap off the rim at the first solid drum roll of trouble. He was completely freaked out by Sarah and me, and the love we now felt for each other, and for Stuart. He was on the outside of that triangle, all alone; and no, there was no other way it might have worked out.

Even from behind, I could tell that Michael was stretched tissue-thin, holding all that fear from the past filled up inside him. But that band holding him together was deteriorating rapidly. That it was going to snap that morning with the power of a slingshot was no revelation for me. I knew him. He was my blood brother. I had seen it coming.

Once I had read his Viet Nam journal, even though it was purely by accident, I knew the truth would have to come out, one way or the other, sooner or later.

But that stinging rubber band had still hit my face as it finally parted and that painful part of Michael's past came pouring out in the form of rage. It was a demon from Michael's past named Drummond that emerged on this particular damp morning.

Michael had never faced what he had done to Drummond, his Green Beret partner. They had shared command and militarily were considered equal in rank and stature. Michael had never been forced, either when it happened, or afterwards, to face the fact that he had killed his best friend, partner, and co-soldier.

Yes, it's true, he had returned to America, and in his own crude, secret, psychological way he had tried to make things right; tried to re-balance the scales, to reconstruct Sarah and Stuart's broken lives with a kind of ultimate selfless effort for justice constructed out of the concept that he could be a replacement husband and father. That somehow he could walk this impossibly loose tightrope between truth and deceit powered purely out of the moral fiber of his own mental being. He had tried to make things right by bandaging, with his own life, the wound he had inflicted.

And so, at this exact moment, with the dawn's sunlight creeping onto the ground like a golden molten metal, I thought about all of these horrible events, all of Michael's grim actions around honor and death, his secret life and his attempts at penance. And then

I realized that what had happened so long ago in that far-off jungle clearing must be brought to a stop here and now, this morning, by me.

I realized that if all the crazy, furious hostility that Michael had brought back to America couldn't be stopped in this Colorado clearing, then it would never be stopped. Violence here would only lead to more violence, and an addiction to pain and endless suffering that would settle in on all our lives and never depart.

So I stopped and I threw my knife down into the mud between us, "If you need to kill me, Michael, go ahead," I said, "but I'm not Drummond, I'm not Anh Dung, and I'm not your own conscience. And, I can't watch you hurt yourself anymore!"

Michael looked at me, his face streaked with mud and blood.

"Drummond made a choice," I went on. "But you made a much more difficult choice—to stop the killing of all those other men. A choice that put you on a path of such pure righteousness that no one could follow you on it. Not even Sarah. A course so pure and empty and desolate that you've been killing yourself, very quietly, but very efficiently, ever since you got back from Viet Nam. And this fight between us is just the final result. Destroy the one person who loves you the most. Because that is the truth: I do love you, and Sarah loves you, and Stuart loves you too. And if you don't realize that, then none of this is worth a good God damn anyway. It is all a waste of time and blood. If you cannot tell that you are loved right this minute, then I have to walk away. I won't watch you destroy yourself anymore, Michael. I'm done. Enough."

I passed my hands very quickly in the air in an "X" pattern, one above the other, to signal that I meant it. The end. My voice shook with the conviction. Then I stood perfectly still and watched Michael's eyes. They gradually fell to where the black handle of my Buck knife harmlessly pierced the soil beside my boot. When his eyes came back up to mine, they were overflowing with tears. Then he let go of his own knife, letting it drop and slice solidly into the ground beside him.

"I'm sorry, Paul. So sorry." He was sobbing now. Tears rolling down his cheeks; old tears, slick and ancient. I had never seen him cry before. "Sorry for everything. Why did Drummond have to do it? Why? Why? It haunts me. He haunts me and I can't fix it." Michael looked at me with a child's pleading eyes.

Stunned at this crack in his bricklike face, I went straight to him with my right arm extended and my hand open and reaching out for him. He grasped it with both of his own hands, clasping my grip desperately, and then using my arm to support himself as his knees buckled.

Slowly, his legs folded up under him and he dropped to his knees. Then, after a beat, he sat slowly back against a log. The adrenaline left him, emptying his rage like water down a drain.

Drenched to the skin, he was already weak and went cold quickly. He began to shiver violently, and then shake uncontrollably. I thought he might be going into shock.

I had to unwrap the viselike grip of his fingers from my hand in order to be able to sit down beside him. Both his hands were still gripping mine. Then carefully I wrapped both my arms around him and pulled him in close to me, lending him all my warmth. I opened my jacket so he could share my body heat. We stayed that way for quite a while and he gradually stopped shaking.

"Are you all right?" I asked finally.

He didn't speak, but nodded that he was. We didn't look at each other as we talked.

"Maybe I should have talked to you about Drummond sooner?" I said, "I don't know."

"I wouldn't have listened," he said. I could see that the creases beside his eyes had lost their pliers-tight grip on his face.

"Thank you, my friend." His voiced cracked. "Thank you for helping me to..."

I waved off his expression of gratitude. We were partners just like the old days again, right away, in that second.

After a few more moments of quiet rest, I helped him to his feet. What had been a raging body only a few minutes ago was now as weak and frail as an old man. Once he was on his feet, he pulled me close again and hugged me. I hugged him back and it almost felt like we were saying goodbye. Then I realized it was as if I was hugging myself, holding that lost and broken part of myself that also needed healing, that part of myself that I had never shown to anyone before meeting Michael and Sarah. I found I couldn't let go of him. I held him with all of my might and he squeezed me back hard.

"Let's find Sarah and Stuart," I said finally, and with our arms around each other we slowly made our way back down to the light and noise of the awakening gathering.

Before we could get back to our campsite, Sarah and Stuart came out of the meadow and found us under the trees.

They had obviously been looking for us, Sarah fearing the worst and looking terribly worried about our recent whereabouts and activities.

Seeing Michael limping along, and obviously in need of assistance, Stuart ran directly to him and grabbed the opposite side from me, curling Michael's arm around his young shoulders and thus making himself a crutch for Michael to lean on. Stuart smiled up at Michael, who smiled back. The boy was more than delighted to support his long-time hero as they slowly trudged back toward the meadow. Stuart's support of Michael was so strong that I could let go of him and I did.

At that point Sarah came up to me and just looked at me, shaking her head. Then she moved in beside me to support me under my right shoulder and got me walking again. I needed her help. I could barely stand after two days of being wide awake, drinking and smoking, and watching or participating in vicious fights. Sarah could also see by my new bruises that there had been more fighting between Michael and me. But she said nothing. In fact, she kissed me softly on a sore spot directly on my cheek.

The dawning sun brought bright orange rays fracturing through the still dark, low-banked clouds of the passing storm front. The radiant rays of magic-hour sunlight, refracted and misty moist, beamed down on our little group and made my friends glow so brightly that it was impossible for me to focus in on any one of them without having to shade my eyes with my hand.

There they were, all shimmering orange like the lustrous peaking embers of a blazing campfire: my best friend, and my love and her child, all now suddenly smiling and hopeful and happy. This change in mood made them all appear natural and beautiful at the same time. All three looked weathered, wind-swept, and gorgeously rugged, as if they had grown right out of the side of the mountain.

A deep happiness came over me, a deep content-ment, because for the first time in my life I thought that maybe I looked that way, too.

Made in the USA
Middletown, DE
19 March 2018